CHURCH OF SHADOWS

BY LEA RYAN

What is a door but a portal to what lies beyond, and who's to say that place isn't populated by stars, filled with fates unknown, or swirling with magic? A door could carry you anywhere.

Chapter 1

At the first turn off County Line 7, the road dipped a little, sending a flutter of anticipation through Tabitha's gut as if she'd just leapt from some precipice. She gripped the wheel tighter to steady herself as the tires of her Blazer hit gravel.

Finally, her research and her waiting were about to pay off. She'd found the perfect place to develop her ability to speak to the dead—a place steeped in history and brimming with whispers of those long gone.

A chill spread across the skin of her right arm, ghostly fingers. She turned to look at the spirit riding shotgun. That day, Giada wore a flapper dress printed with little flowers, her hair in pin curls. Her lips, a deep, dark color against her translucent skin, curled into a reassuring smile.

"I'm fine," Tabitha insisted. "I have to be."

Everything she'd worked for hinged on this little church out in the middle of nowhere. All the nights she'd gone out with the ghost hunting teams, all the reading she'd done, the shadow work, they'd trained her for this, the real deal. If she couldn't connect with spirits while living in one of the most notoriously-haunted properties in the state, she didn't know what else to do.

So far, despite all the work, she'd only connected with one spirit: Giada, a woman who died in the 1920s after losing her infant daughter. Tabitha had learned much, but what good was a medium who could only connect with one spirit? It would never get her childhood friend back.

Her phone buzzed in the drink holder, but she ignored it, as she had all day. The messages were from her ex, Philip, who hadn't taken the breakup well. When she stopped, she'd double-check that the locator app was finally gone from her phone. What once felt like a harmless way to check each other's ETA for dinner had become another tool for his relentless stalking.

On their right, a driveway cut through a lawn that had gone to prairie in front of a small, gray farmhouse. No doubt they had some stories to tell, living so close to the property previously owned by Orrin Riley and his death cult.

Then she was at the edge of her destination, passing the realty sign, turning onto the property that practically radiated the energy of tragedy. The exterior of the church looked pristine, trimmed bushes at the base of white clapboard siding, blood-red shutters on the windows. An octagonal bell tower reminded her more of a lighthouse than a church steeple, a lighthouse in a forest.

"I hope the bell still works." She grinned over at Giada, who was staring up at the place, wide-eyed, seemingly afraid. "What's wrong?"

Tabitha's phone went off again, the buzz sound grating. She probably should've broken up with Philip sooner. Maybe dumping him and then immediately leaving town was a bad idea, after all. He still would've tried to come after her, but maybe he wouldn't have been as angry.

Giada spoke in her airy, faraway voice. "You can't hear them?"

Tabitha put down the window and cocked her head. Nothing but a few birds and the rustle of an autumn breeze through the shadowy trees. She shook her head.

"It's a hum like...bees but human voices, many of them, men, women rising and falling like waves." Giada sat back in her seat as if to put distance between her and the church. "This is a mistake. We should go."

"But look how excited she is."

The grinning realtor waited for them at the top of the front steps, clutching a folder to her chest with one hand and waving frantically with the other. She looked just like her photo from the realtor website, perfectly curled golden hair, classic makeup, even the same lavender skirt suit, the very picture of real estate professionalism.

Tabitha was glad people didn't expect that from her. She couldn't imagine having to work a job that required you to bind yourself in clothes that looked like they were made more of starch than fabric. She preferred clothes she could move in, frayed jeans, artfully-distressed designer-wear that flowed around her.

She tied her tangle of blonde and brown waves into a loose ponytail and said, "We'll be okay. I mean, you're already dead. What's the worst that could happen?"

Giada's expression morphed into anger. Being dead was one thing. Being reminded you were dead was another.

Tabitha sighed. "I apologize. That was rude of me. You can stay in the car if you want or take off. I won't try and force you into something you don't want to do."

The ghost's annoyance abated. "You already know I'll stay with you, kiddo."

"Yeah, I know. Come on. I'll protect you."

As Tabitha got out of the car, she caught a chill and pulled on the faux fur coat from the back seat. The temperature here seemed lower than it should've been, given the sunshine and the weather.

Helen of the lavender skirt suit jabbed her hand between them as Tabitha reached the top of the stairs. "I am so excited to finally meet you in person, Ms. Mainwater. I've admired your work for years." She handed over a packet of information about the place.

Time to do the public relations dance. Over the course of the last few years, Tabitha's work had gained popularity throughout the state. People didn't always recognize her, but enough did that she'd grown accustomed to the attention and the responses that her brain had practically automated.

"Thank you. That's so kind of you to say."

"My mother has already set aside funds for you to paint her once she passes on. She does have to wait, right? I mean, she might pay extra if she gets to see it."

This was a common request and one Tabitha never granted. She had a few excuses she liked to give, most of them with some spiritual angle, her go-to being that the muse wouldn't speak to her unless the person's spirit had crossed over. The real reason she didn't paint the living was that she didn't want them to complain about the way she painted their likeness.

Can you remove that mole? Can you slim my jawline, arms, waist just a tad? Can you just smooth some of my wrinkles? She didn't have the time or patience for any of it.

"I do apologize, but my gift only allows me to paint those who have passed. I'm afraid they must become true angels before I can paint them in that form."

"Oh." Helen's smile faltered, but she recovered quickly. She waved off the apology. "No problem. Are you ready to see the house?" She laughed and opened the door. "Church? Church house? Heck, I don't know."

Inside, the lingering scent of melted wax from legions of candles hit Tabitha with a kind of weight that settled in her chest. Sunlight poured through the tall windows as if trying to cleanse the dark past.

The house flippers had sectioned off the sanctuary into an open floor plan that included a kitchen with long, granite counters and an island immediately to the left of the entrance and a living room further in, the sofa facing a wall, where they'd hung a big screen television.

To the right was an office nook, complete with a large, antique desk and bookshelves Tabitha wouldn't mind keeping. But the real point of interest lay straight ahead, where an altar once stood. The only remnant of its presence was a decorative arch that soared toward the high ceiling, its topmost point nearly brushing the rafters

The wall there was the same white as the rest of them, but there was something vacuous about the space where the large crucifix once hung. Before she knew what was happening, she had moved a few steps toward it and away from Helen, who was desperately trying to direct her toward the kitchen.

Tabitha cleared her throat and said, "Just absorbing the vibe of the place."

She closed her eyes and breathed in the scent of candles once more. The air was thick in her lungs but not unpleasantly, and it calmed her, somehow. She'd visited plenty of haunted places. None of them felt like this. None of them seemed to wrap arms around her and welcome her the way this place did. What did that mean?

If she listened closely enough, what would the old walls say? Would she hear screaming or rejoicing? Perhaps both?

Giada appeared at her side, bringing a faint chill and the smell of frost with her. She leaned in close, as if Realtor Helen might actually hear her.

"You're inviting them?"

"It's what we're here for, right?"

"Not now. Not yet."

Tabitha was about to reply when she saw Helen leaning against the kitchen island, staring.

What did Helen think of her, dressed head-to-toe in hippie-wear and standing at the center of the haunted church, soaking up the energy where people died violently? She probably looked like some kind of new age lunatic, possibly a new member for the long-gone cult.

"Right," Tabitha said. "Moving on."

Helen was all too happy to get on with her spiel. "The most recent update is the apron sink in the kitchen." She presented it with pride, as if she'd installed it herself.

The rest of the tour went on as it would have with any other property. Helen was awfully cheery, given the history. A pair of bedrooms occupied the upstairs loft overlooking the sanctuary, and Tabitha paused there to take in the view. The profound, sunlit beauty of the place reached within her, touching the longing she'd carried since Rebecca died all those years ago. This was exactly what she needed to come into her own, assuming the spirits cooperated.

"Well, we've seen all the good parts inside. Would you like to see the rest of the property? There's an old pole barn in the back that would make a perfect studio with a little sprucing up."

"I'd like to see the basement, please."

At the bottom of the loft stairs, Helen hesitated, clutching her folder tighter. "Of course. This way." She led them around the corner, past the kitchen.

"Is something wrong with the basement?"

"No. Well, maybe. It's just not one of the best selling points."

"I'm no expert, but aren't real estate agents supposed to show the entire property?"

"You're right. My apologies."

Giada stayed with Tabitha, eager but unwilling to move ahead of her. The closer they got to the big, metal door, the graver her expression became. She shot glances at the corners, at the ceiling and the shadows, as if trying to pinpoint the source of a sound. Tabitha was dying to ask her questions, but that would have to wait.

At the basement door, Helen took a deep breath before pulling the handle. Inside, an overhead light flickered to life, the illumination weak and pale, spilling down the walls at odd angles. The stairs were new.

"If you'd like to take a quick look around, I'm just going to wait here." Helen offered up a nervous smile. Giada moved to stand next to her as if in solidarity, and the realtor shivered and hugged her arms.

"What's wrong with the basement?" Tabitha asked.

"Last time I was down there, I got a little spooked."

"Did you see something?"

Helen gave a nervous laugh. "I'd rather not say."

"Whatever you tell me, I'll believe you."

Helen demurred, shaking her head and shrugging. "It's nothing. I..."

Heavy silence fell between them, Tabitha pressing the point with a look. Helen seemed on the verge of tears.

A heavy object slammed to the floor in the basement, startling all three women.

Tabitha asked, "Is someone down there?"

"Not that I know of." She was about to bolt; Tabitha could feel it. "I'll check it out."

As Tabitha stepped toward the doorway, Helen gripped her arm. "What if it's a burglar?"

"All the way out here?" She took another step, but Helen held on, trembling.

"Or an animal? It might be a rabid raccoon. We should call the police or animal control, maybe both." Her words were hushed and desperate.

Tabitha gently removed Helen's hand. "How about I go see what it is, and you stay here, and I'll tell you who to call?"

"But the liability—"

"I'm not going to sue you. Stay here."

Giada had vanished, which was strange. Tabitha repressed an urge to call out for her friend, lest she freak out Helen any further. She was on her own with this one.

Lightbulbs daisy-chained by unsafe looking wiring trailed down the sloping ceiling. The first few stairs creaked underfoot, but they seemed sturdy enough, newer than the church itself, perhaps installed by the house flippers.

The real estate listing had included a single picture of the basement. To anyone who didn't know the history of the church, it probably just looked like a musty, old office with a couple of small storage rooms at the back.

Tabitha knew better. This was where the worst of it happened. This was where Orrin kept the followers who struggled with their faith. His power still stifled the air, a kind of control that remained long after his death.

A heavy, metal desk sat at the center of the main room, facing the bottom of the stairs. The light fixture over it swayed slowly in a breeze she couldn't feel.

"Giada?" she whispered. "Are you here?"

Silence.

Swallowing the knot in her throat, she descended into the basement. Moldering boxes slumped against one another, against the walls, their contents barely contained. Spare parts from previous renovations mingled with them, lengths of pipe in one corner, forgotten boxes of tile in another.

Near the bit of hallway between the storage rooms, a pair of olive green filing cabinets stood watch. How could anyone use this as a workspace? Did they not know what happened here?

An ominous stain spread from beneath the filing cabinet to her left. She insisted to herself that it couldn't be blood. Whoever cleaned the church after the tragedy had done such a thorough job. They wouldn't have forgotten something so blatant...unless they were too afraid to work in the basement.

Pressure formed in her chest, worsening the closer she got to the storage rooms. Then came the sensation of what she could only describe as wanting. The energy of this place caused her pain. Yet, she couldn't stop herself from moving toward it.

Between the storerooms, the concrete floor rooted her to where she stood. Her own ragged breath the only sound in her ears, Tabitha couldn't move. Something, someone had ensnared her.

A stench of blood stung her nostrils. She closed her eyes. This wasn't real.

"Tell me your fears, your dreams. Together, we can explore it all." A man's voice sounded from another room, somewhere upstairs in the church, where a murmur passed through a crowd that wasn't really there.

From the storage room on the left came a delicate scratching on the concrete floor. Tabitha's pulse raced harder. She found her fingers, curled them into a fist.

More scratching, a whisper across the floor, this time closer. Whatever made the sound was approaching.

She wanted to run away. She wanted to remain and witness. She wanted both and neither because knowledge could change everything in an instant.

A small, brown rabbit hopped into view, into the middle of the hallway. It sat for a moment, nose twitching, and then it turned to look at her with bottomless, black eyes.

Behind her, the metal door to the basement slammed, the sound of it echoing. And though she couldn't turn to watch, she felt the daisy-chained light bulbs go dark, one by one with soft pops, giving way to a chilling void that spread behind her. It closed in until all that remained was the singular light fixture over the desk.

"Let go." Her whisper to the room was the loudest sound she could make.

Her phone buzzed in her hand, breaking the spell. She squealed and dropped it, and the phone clattered across the floor. Instead of pulsing like it usually did, the vibration persisted. It intensified as if trying to rattle the phone apart. Tabitha snatched it up, gripping it hard to hold it steady enough for her to read the screen.

Philip. She should've known. Text messages scrolled up the screen, rapid-fire, a handheld marquee of rage. Demands to know her location. Demands to meet and discuss their dead relationship. Why did she abandon him? *Bitch. How could you?*

"Stop," she said, this command stronger than the last she'd given the room.

The words faded. The screen fell dark.

Tabitha looked back toward the rabbit. It was gone. The lights behind her shone as if nothing had happened. The door at the top of the stairs stood open. Helen was gone.

She found the realtor out on the driveway, one hand on her knee, the other on the driver's side door of her red sedan. The folder lay at her feet, the papers, pictures of the church, lists of its amenities and improvements, were scattered across the gravel, corners turning up in the afternoon breeze.

"Are you alright?" Tabitha ran over. "What did you see?"

Helen was breathing hard. "The door. It closed by itself. On the way out, I thought I saw a...a woman in a dress."

Giada. As far as Tabitha knew, no one but her could see Giada.

Breathless, Helen added, "I couldn't hear her, but her face looked like she was screaming."

Tabitha glanced back at the door to the church. It stood open, waiting for her return.

"I'll be right back," she assured Helen, who tried to make a grab for her arm again.

Inside, Tabitha called out for Giada. She searched the sanctuary, the bedrooms. She looked down the basement stairs but no longer felt a presence down there.

"Giada?" She beckoned from the bottom of the loft stairs, and then turned, and Giada was there, smiling sweetly. "Are you okay? Where did you go?"

Giada looked confused and then shrugged.

"She saw you. Do you know why?"

"No, she didn't."

"She just said she saw a woman in a dress."

"Another woman, I'm sure."

Tabitha narrowed her eyes. Something about this didn't seem right. She'd let it go for now, but there would be more questions later.

When she returned, Helen was frantically gathering her paperwork from the driveway. Tabitha moved to help.

"Thank you," Helen said. "Honestly, I am so sorry I ran out. I must be tired. This might be a stupid question, but what did you think?"

"I'll take it."

Chapter 2

Two Months Later

A knock at the front door interrupted Tabitha's tea. She got up from her stool at the kitchen island to answer, prepared to meet the plumber she'd spoken to on the phone about her leaky kitchen faucet. Judging by the sound of him, she'd guessed him at about 75 years old.

She blocked the bright, midmorning sun with her hand to get a better look at the man on her porch. He was not 75. He was tall, rugged good looks with hair likely faded by the sun and a beard to match. Clad in a flannel shirt, jeans, and hiking boots, the scent of the forest clung to him. He did not look prepared to fix a faucet.

"Good morning, ma'am. Name's Lucas McGuire. I'm your neighbor to the south." He tipped his head that direction. "Heard you bought the place."

Tabitha shook hands with him. His palm was warm and worn by work. He looked strong and earthy, very unlike her ex. She found herself reluctant to release his hand.

A dog sat at his feet, a short, chubby speckled dog with a narrow face. Lucas added, "And this is Jackal."

"Nice to meet you. Tabitha Mainwater."

"Nice to meet you." His smile was broad and genuine. He tipped his head again, this time to peer into the house behind her. "You need help with anything? Heavy boxes or..." He stopped as a truck with a pipe wrench logo painted on the side rolled to a stop on the gravel driveway.

The man who got out of it was about 75, and his coveralls looked nearly as old. They were streaked with grease, almost as dirty as the red toolbox he hauled out of the passenger seat with him. She and Lucas waited as he made his way to the steps.

"Mornin', ma'am. I'm here about the faucet."

Zeke. His name tag matched the name painted on the truck. Owner. Operator. Plumber. He walked with a limp and nodded a greeting at Lucas as he reached the steps.

"Zeke." Lucas returned the nod. "How's Gertie?"

"Fine, baking brownies with a few ladies from church. Thanks for askin'."

Tabitha moved to show him to the faucet in question. To her surprise, Lucas followed them inside. He hadn't asked, and she hadn't invited.

"You're Mrs. Mainwater," Zeke said.

She smiled. "Ms. but yes."

He looked her over appraisingly and then nodded solemnly. "Should have it fixed in a jiff. Probably just a valve." With that, he bent down and went to work.

Lucas tapped Tabitha on the shoulder. "Can I talk to you for a minute?"

She nodded, and he led her several feet away. He kept his voice low. "I realize you haven't been here long, but have you seen anything strange?"

She considered lying. She wasn't obligated to tell him anything. This was her private property and her business.

"Strange like men barging their way in with the plumber?"

"This place...well, I'm sure you knew something about it before you bought it."

"That a cult used to operate out of the church?"

"Live here long enough, and you'll realize that 'cult' is too simple a word for what happened to these people and to this land."

"I bought this place because I needed a fresh start. Maybe it needs one, too."

He narrowed his eyes. "That the only reason?"

"The only reason that's any of your business."

He nodded slowly in understanding. "You bought it *because* it's haunted."

She hated how easily he'd read her. They'd known each other for all of thirty seconds.

"You should probably go."

"Why?"

"Because you're prying, and that's rude."

"I just want to make sure you're safe is all. The spirits here might cause you some problems."

"What kind of problems?"

"The soul-wrecking kind."

Tabitha started to show him toward the door, leading him gently by the arm. "I appreciate your concern, but I can take care of myself."

"Look, I can see you're busy, but we need to talk. I know more about this place than what you read." He pivoted to stand between her and the door but kept walking backward toward it. "Can I come by later?"

The prospect of more information did intrigue her. Maybe she'd learn something useful. But she needed to get her bearings first, get the feel of the place, at the very least. Besides, in her experience, small town people didn't always like when strangers moved to town. He might be trying to scare her off for whatever reason.

"Maybe in a few days after I unpack."

He nodded, his concern still evident. "Alright then, Ms. Mainwater. Take care."

As she watched Lucas and Jackal head down the driveway, she hoped he wouldn't make trouble for her. She had enough problems with Philip still hounding her. All she needed was another man causing her grief. Tabitha closed the door.

Chapter 3

A pair of large oil paintings leaned against the base of the archway at the front of the sanctuary. At her request, the movers had left her two favorite paintings near the part of the room that had once held an altar and still held that fantastic arch. She wanted to hang them as soon as possible, not just because she was afraid they'd get damaged. If the church was going to feel like home, those paintings needed to be on the wall.

Tabitha specialized in Renaissance-style paintings of angels. Dark backgrounds, deep, rich color, eyes sometimes turned Heavenward.

The first painting, the one on the left, was of her father, the way he looked when he was young, before the cancer took him. In that painting, he was bent over his workbench, hand carving detail into a chunk of wood in a vice.

Instead of the usual white angel wings, she'd given him feathers in earthy shades of brown and red speckled here and there in white. They were the wings of a red-tailed hawk, a bird he often pointed out when he took her hiking.

The second painting was inspired by a far older wound and one that shaped much of how she'd come to view mortality and the fragility of life. The subject of that painting was the reason she'd become a medium in the first place.

Everything seemed to circle back to her long-dead childhood friend, Rebecca. She was eight years old when she died, forever eight years old in this painted angelic version of her, a halo around her golden brown waves of hair.

Tabitha's obsession with the dead began the moment the chill of that loss seeped into her bones. Death, once a distant shadow, became an intimate companion. She could no longer accept that Rebecca was gone; she needed to know, to feel, that her soul still burned brightly, somewhere out there.

That evening, Tabitha was unpacking yet another box when she heard a thud from the bedroom in the loft above her. Giada turned, frowning. The vinyl album of soft piano music went on playing, suddenly eerie in the stillness.

"Something fell," Tabitha assured her friend and herself. Except for the bed, she'd focused her unpacking efforts on the first floor. In the loft, boxes and random junk were stacked precariously against the walls.

Giada stared up at the loft, ghostly brow furrowed. A door upstairs clicked closed, and they both jumped.

"Something fell and rolled into the door?" Tabitha asked.

Giada shook her head no. Then she got up to check it out. She vanished in a wisp of mist.

The piano music continued playing. Outside, the wind whispered warnings against the clapboard siding as the black night sky watched through the tall church windows.

Nearby, on a box, her phone buzzed. She picked it up to look at the screen. The display flickered and died in her hand.

Philip's voice sounded from somewhere among the stacks of boxes around her. "God damn it, Tabitha. If you'd just listen to me, do what I tell you, everything will be perfect."

Not possible. Her breath quickened, and she searched for a weapon, her eyes landing on a box cutter. Greedily, she snatched it from the floor, held it out between her and whoever, whatever might come.

"He's not here." She considered running, but where would she go?

"I am wherever you are, always, because we are meant to be. Now, if you'd just listen. All you have to do is everything for me. Prove your love. We can be happy." Philip never talked that way. He had wanted those things, yes, but his tone was always sharper, his words more cutting.

She searched among the boxes, her movements the only sign of life in the stillness. He wasn't there. She remembered her experience in the basement, how the spirits had used her fear of her ex to communicate.

"Can I see you?" she asked the spirit. "Please. I'm not afraid."

A different man laughed, his voice distant but also, somehow, next to her. Something reached for her from beyond the veil, a yearning so potent that it tugged at her soul.

He spoke. "You are so much more than you think you are. In death, we are all gods." Now, this tone was that of someone preaching, not speaking directly to her. It was an echo from the past.

She'd never been this close to making direct contact with any spirits other than Giada. For so long, she'd had to satisfy her need to commune with the dead through recorded shadows and disembodied voices muttering in the dark.

This presence was more powerful than any that she'd felt. It was no ordinary lost soul. She felt him standing behind her. She wheeled around to find nothing.

"I'm not afraid."

At the archway, a set of white double doors shimmered into existence, ghostly reflections of the church's front entrance. Ivy coiled around the edges, dark tendrils creeping from the center, as if something from beyond was pushing through, desperate to breach the fragile boundary between their world and this one.

As if caught in a slow but deadly undertow of spiritual energy, she drifted toward the doors, barely aware of the sensation of the box cutter slipping from her fingers. Whatever lay beyond those doors tugged at her soul with promises of knowing and magic, something far beyond mortal comprehension.

Tears warmed her face, flowing freely as she slowly, agonizingly slowly, closed the immeasurable distance between her and the loving arms of this miracle. Death could be nothing. Death could be everything.

"Let me go." In her desperation, she barely found the words.

"Patience," the man said, his voice sultry and inviting. "I can give you everything, but only if you first understand the depth of the offering I ask of you."

Energy pulsed through her, giving rise to sensations of yearning, desire, bottomless need like she'd never felt before. Without this, without him, she was but an empty vessel.

"What's on the other side?"

"Everything you've ever wanted." Again, he stood behind her.

Then she was right in front of the doors, reaching for the handles.

Intense cold bloomed along her upper arms, a grip that yanked her back.

"Wait!" she shouted and reached, but the doors were gone. Tabitha spun around to find Giada standing behind her. "Why? Why would you do that? I was so close."

"You're being reckless."

"Reckless? You know how hard I've worked for this."

"These spirits mean harm. We shouldn't be here."

"No one is keeping you here, Giada. Go if you need to."

With that, Giada vanished.

Tabitha turned back to the archway. "She's gone." Nothing happened. She waited. "Please."

But she was alone.

Chapter 4

That night, she dreamed of Orrin, the charismatic leader of the Church of Ascendants. She dreamed of his voice and knew he was the one who'd spoken to her in the sanctuary. He was the one who promised miracles with such confidence that it smoothed the rough edges of her self-doubt.

He left her a gift.

The next morning, a small, square box waited at the bottom of the stairs. Corners crumpled and the cardboard water-stained, she could tell immediately that it wasn't one of hers.

She took it to the kitchen counter and unfolded the flaps. Inside, she found black and white photographs of Orrin dressed in a suit with his cult, most of them looking happy, men and women holding drinks at parties. An unexpected pang of envy hit her at the sight of their physical proximity to him.

She shook her head. This was getting ridiculous. She couldn't allow herself to obsess over a dead man, especially one who was actively haunting her. That was dangerous in a number of ways.

More serious photos showed them sitting at tables, among stacks of books, scribbling notes. One showed them several people dressed in white wrappings that barely covered their bodies as they danced around a large bonfire.

There were journals and sketches in the box as well. Brittle pages featured planetary diagrams interspersed with symbols. The journals contained pages and pages of handwriting from different people, accounts of conversations with someone named "Cernunnos." On several of the pages, the writing started as strong but then faltered toward the end, occasionally ending in a line that dragged to the edge of the paper.

Orrin wrote about the nature of the soul, its energy, the kind of light he thought it might be made of. Tabitha had watched a documentary on Orrin's cult long before she bought the place. The documentarians made him seem like a madman and a murderer, someone cruel and meant to be feared. These writings painted a different picture.

His philosophies were perfectly coherent and well-thought-out. He approached his work with an almost scientific mind. He documented his attempts to communicate with the spirit world better than she had. She realized they had a lot in common.

Giada appeared faint that morning as she sat at the kitchen island with Tabitha. Her ghostly green presence was barely visible. Even stranger, she kept cocking her head and glancing around the room as if trying to pinpoint the source of a noise.

"What's wrong?" Tabitha finally asked.

"Nothing."

"What do you hear?"

"It's just my imagination."

"I don't think it is your imagination."

"It's just..." Giada looked down at her hands folded in her lap. "A cat somewhere, perhaps?"

"A cat?" Tabitha closed her eyes and listened but heard nothing but the autumn wind. "I don't hear it."

"I told you." Giada gave her an uncertain smile.

Tabitha changed the subject. "I'm sorry I snapped at you last night. I know you were trying to help."

"It's alright."

"I want you to know, though, that I don't plan to stop."

"I know."

"Orrin isn't what I thought he was. His power is unlike anything I've ever seen."

"Men use power to corrupt and control."

"And if contact with him makes me stronger?"

Giada shrugged.

"Whatever this is, I need you to let me explore it."

"I don't want anything to happen to you."

"Something happens to all of us eventually. The answers I've been looking for are in this church. Giada, this is my chance. Even if it looks dangerous, I have to push forward. Please tell me you understand."

Her reluctance evident, Giada nodded and then vanished. Tabitha sighed. She didn't want to have to choose between her friend and this place. Of all the people who might discourage her, she never suspected Giada would become one of them.

Tabitha's thoughts circled back to Rebecca. The memory that remained most vivid in her mind was an angel doll that Rebecca brought to school the week before she died, the porcelain face and the vivid bottle-green glass eyes. One of the boys in class took it and broke it, and to their horror, the inside of the doll's face was painted a deep crimson.

Rebecca had cried just as any other girl with a broken doll might have, but all Tabitha felt was dread. Later, next to the gravel road where he broke the doll, she pushed the boy over and over, pretending that her anger was greater than the fear. Why would anyone paint the inside of a doll the color of blood?

The next week, on the other side of the playground, Rebecca ran after a ball that rolled into the street. Then came the squeal of brakes and tires and the terrible thump and blood spreading across the pavement. More red, another broken doll. It was the last thing she remembered before the darkness and the numbness took her.

But this place had offered her a door. To what, though?

And what if she did find Rebecca on the other side of the spirit door? If the door led to the spirit world, would Tabitha want to come back? Or would she remain there and let the world think she was dead?

From the bottom of the box, she pulled out a daguerreotype, a picture of Orrin. He was dapper in a suit, his hair a little wild. He stared at the camera with pale, almost spectral eyes, seemingly at her, a secret playing across his lips in a mischievous smile.

He didn't look like a villain. He didn't look evil. In fact, she liked his face, the angle of his jaw, the proud way he held himself. If they met in life, he was someone she might've liked, certainly someone she would've been attracted to.

She turned over the daguerreotype.

May 7, 1844. An impossible date, given that Orrin died in 1942 at the supposed age of 39.

Tabitha turned the thing over and over in her hand, trying to figure out what this meant. Was it even real? Maybe it was one of those old-fashioned tourist photos that looked older than they were. Did those exist in the 40s?

Before she could begin to understand this thing, she needed to know if it was real. She needed an expert.

Chapter 5

Beneath a sky shrouded in heavy, churning clouds, Tabitha climbed into the Blazer. As she cranked the heat to ward off the chill and set the GPS to an antique store in downtown Jericho, she thought of Orrin again and his promises and the sensation of his voice in her ear. It was easy to see why people followed him. He possessed a kind of supernatural magnetism that she, for one, found irresistible. She would have to be careful.

Small towns in Indiana all seemed to follow a similar format. They had the requisite old-fashioned hardware store, the boutiques selling clothes and fancy gifts in country decorating schemes. Restaurants were either small chains or locally owned. Even the architecture shared DNA with just a few notable details to set them apart.

All of this was fine with her. They had a way of always feeling like home.

Grueller's Antique shop lay nestled between an equally ancient-looking bookstore and a newer t-shirt printing place that had tie-dyed t-shirts hanging in the windows.

A brass bell above the antique store door rang as she entered. The interior was warm and smelled of old paper and dust in a way that she loved. Music played, too, an old recording of Casey Kasem's Top 40 playing over speakers mounted in the corners of the room, accompanied by the ticking of many clocks.

Shelves were packed to the gills with trinkets and dishes that gleamed in the low light, some of them arranged by color and theme. Buckets of architectural bits like door hardware and wooden trim were clustered more haphazardly, as if someone wasn't sure how to organize them. She could've spent all day exploring the place, but she had business to attend to.

A gray-haired man smiled as she approached the counter. "Morning. How can I help you?"

Tabitha fished through her bag for the daguerreotype. "I was wondering if someone here could help me verify the authenticity of this."

He put on reading glasses as she handed it over. He took one look at it, put it down on the counter, and walked away.

"Juney!" He called out. "You got a cult crazy out here."

"I'm not a cult crazy," Tabitha muttered to herself and pouted but then wondered if that was true.

A middle-aged hippie woman who bore an uncanny resemblance to John Lennon emerged from behind a beaded curtain in a doorway. She smiled at Tabitha. "Sorry about Miles. His whole life is a mood. What have we got?" She picked up the daguerreotype. "Orrin Riley. Nice looking guy. Too bad about the murderiness of it all." She turned it over to look at the back. "Where did you get this?"

"I found it in a box of his things. I bought the church."

Juney looked at Tabitha over her glasses. "You bought the church?"

"Yes. I live there."

"Whoo, lady, you are surely a special one. Bad mojo in that place, but it's your funeral, I guess." She shrugged and squinted at the picture. "Well, your daguerreotype looks authentic as far as I can tell. The date doesn't make sense."

"He would've been well over a century old when he died."

"While looking exactly the same," Juney finished. "Could be a relative."

"That's possible."

"You could go through the trouble of mapping out Orrin's family tree and figuring out which relative that is, but given that his origins are a bit of a mystery, you might have some trouble with that. There have been rumors, but no one has been able to find a record of him before he opened his church." Juney handed the daguerreotype back to her. "So are you a researcher, a ghost hunter, or a cult crazy?" Juney asked.

"None of the above." She thought for a moment and changed her mind. "I guess you could consider me a ghost hunter, just not the kind you might be thinking of. I'm a medium."

"Oh, lord. That is so much worse." Juney rubbed her forehead with her fingertips. "I had an aunt who was sensitive to psychic energy. She swore she heard voices of the dead, which wasn't a big deal for a while. People ignored her or laughed behind her back until the voices started telling her to do things. And when she started following their orders, that was when she ended up in the nuthouse."

"Noted." Tabitha dropped the daguerreotype into her bag and turned to go.

"Does Lucas McGuire still live out there?"

"Yes. He's my neighbor."

"His family has owned that farm for generations. He'd be the closest thing you have to an expert. I'm not sure how much help he might be with the picture, but I'm sure he could answer some questions for you."

Great. Mr. Invite-Himself-In. She hated to admit it, but Juney was probably right.

Chapter 6

Later that afternoon, back at the church, workmen came to hang the paintings of her father and Rebecca at the front of the church, above the spot where the ghostly door had appeared the previous night. They offered excellent advice about the proper height of paintings for decorating purposes, which she appreciated, and part of her wanted to explain her strange reasoning. But she let it go, content to let them think she was stubborn.

Now, her oil-painted dead watched with soulful eyes as Tabitha sat at the kitchen island with Orrin's photos and writings spread out across the countertop. She traced his pen marks, feeling the imprint of his touch radiating through the years. These were his dreams, his reality. She envisioned long nights spent over pen and paper as he wrote out these teachings for his followers.

Flawed as his ideals were, she couldn't help but acknowledge this power was real. Much like the spirit of the man himself, it defied death.

Not all of his writings were in English. Some of it looked like Latin, but there was another language that she couldn't place.

The writing looked like the English alphabet. It was the arrangement of letters that threw her, the words. A search on her phone yielded no results. Could Orrin have made up a language or some sort of code?

One name stood out to her. It appeared over and over. "Cernunnos." It had significance.

She searched the internet for Orrin and the other name. Nothing came up. She searched the name by itself, but every result was garbled, the link leading to a page that could not be found.

"Curiouser and curiouser," she muttered.

She remembered Juney's suggestion and rolled her eyes at the thought. Would her neighbor, Lucas, even tell her anything? Would he give her information or just serve up more ominous warnings about her soul?

The sky outside the church windows had started to tip toward evening. If she planned to walk over and return by dark, she had to leave quickly. She groaned and put on her coat and a scarf, drawing up her hood as she stepped outside to lock the door.

Tabitha headed the way he had on the first day he came to visit, the opening in the trees, figuring that if he and his dog had walked over, it couldn't be that far. She made a left from her driveway, where she immediately found a worn dirt path.

As she made her way in the fading light and fallen leaves, a disturbing idea occurred to her. Not only was she venturing into the woods alone, she didn't know if Lucas was dangerous. Her tumultuous past with her abusive ex had shaken her confidence in her ability to read people. Would she know a killer if she met one?

Near the other end of the path, music reached her, coming from behind the house. She went that way instead of toward the front door, and she found the source: a speaker set up on the back porch, blasting "Looking Out My Back Door" by Creedence Clearwater Revival.

Behind the house, what looked like prairie spanned wide and far into the distance, weeds and wildflowers withering in pale shades of death and vibrant shades of rust. Tabitha had heard this was supposed to be a farm. It didn't look like Lucas McGuire grew anything but prairie.

Down a dirt path that ran along the edge of the trees between his property and the church, she found him hacking away at a vine. The machete in his hand gave her pause. Tabitha kept her distance as she made her presence known.

"Mr. McGuire?"

He didn't hear her, only kept up his chopping. Jackal, his dog, turned to look at her, wagging his tail. She said Lucas' name again, louder, and that time, he heard her.

He looked up and grinned. Round, welding goggles covered his eyes, and a lit joint hung from his mouth, the smell of it potent in the clear, cool air.

"Hey. What can I do for you, neighbor lady?"

"What are you doing?"

"Landscaping?" he said and then laughed. He dropped the vine and rose to stand, the machete still in his hand. He removed the joint from his mouth. "I'd appreciate it if you kept your paranormal entities on your side of the property line."

"What?"

"The ivy." He traded the machete for a small bottle of whiskey sitting on the ground.

"Are you drunk?"

"Well, yes, but that doesn't invalidate my request." His words had more of a country twang than before, probably the result of the weed and the whiskey.

"What do my paranormal entities have to do with your yard?"

"Honey, everything. You never answered my question. What can I do for you?" He smirked like he knew exactly why she was there.

"What do you know about Cernunnos?"

The grin fell from his face. "Never heard of him."

"Him? How do you know it's a 'him?'"

Lucas shook his head. "Some secrets, it's best they stay secret so they don't gain new life. You understand?"

"No. Was Cernunnos one of Orrin's followers?"

"People like you think this is a game. These entities are dangerous. Orrin is dangerous. His followers are dangerous. Cernunnos is the most dangerous thing of all. I won't mention his name again, and neither should you. Now, if you'll excuse me, I have more supernatural nonsense to trim back." He took a long swig off the bottle that made him sway on his feet.

Silence fell between them, and the music from his porch reached her again. Night was coming on fast, and she needed to get home.

She said, "This isn't a game to me. I've lost people. I'm just trying to make contact with them. I want them back." The tremble in her voice surprised her.

Lucas softened a little. "I sympathize, but this isn't the way to do it. If I thought I could get my parents back through Orrin, I would've tried years ago. None of this is what you think it is. I've seen the documentaries. Trust me when I say they left out the worst parts."

"They covered the deaths."

"I know what they covered. Death isn't the worst thing that can happen to a person. Stay in that church, and you'll find out the hard way."

Tabitha switched tracks. If he wouldn't answer that one, maybe she could get him to answer a simpler one.

"How old was Orrin, really? Do you know?"

"Older than he should've been. Go on home, now, before the darkness catches up."

"Thanks." Disappointed, she turned to go. He stopped her one last time.

"You can call me 'Lucas,' by the way. We're neighbors now, for a little while, at least."

"Right. Tabitha."

"Noted!" He saluted as he put down the whiskey to retrieve the machete.

Back up the dirt road, past the speaker on the porch that now blasted "Bad Moon Rising," into the field, a feeling of dread followed Tabitha. Deep down, she knew he was right, knew that none of this felt safe to know or talk about, but she needed it. Every piece of the puzzle was important. Every piece provided context she needed if she would find a way back to her friend.

"No matter what," she vowed to herself.

Chapter 7

Tabitha set up her easel near the archway at the front of the sanctuary. The paintings of Rebecca and her father always warmed her to the deceased person she was painting at any given time. Whenever she felt herself slipping emotionally, she would look up at those two paintings (arguably her best work) to remind herself what her subject meant to the people who loved them.

Tonight's subject was Ms. Mina Frances Dellin, an older woman, who died of a stroke in her home but not before she commissioned her own angel portrait from Tabitha. Most of the time, relatives commissioned paintings once the subjects had passed on. Her wealthier clients commissioned their own. Nothing enabled someone to secure a legacy quite like a boatload of money.

Giada appeared a couple of hours later, looking confused. She started near the entrance of the church, scanning the room as she made her way to Tabitha.

"Hey, lady. I missed you today. Are you okay?"

"Sure, kiddo."

Her dress, a dark, flapper number with fringes, hung strangely on her body, off kilter at the waist as if her torso were somehow misaligned by an inch or two. Her visual appearance, her clothing especially, served as a reflection of her mood. As before, she cocked her head as if listening.

"What do you hear?"

She offered up a dazzling smile. "Nothing. How was your day?"

Tabitha narrowed her eyes. "Alright." She thought for a moment and then asked, "Have you ever heard of Cernunnos?"

"Never," she said, obviously a lie. She was terrified.

"Then why do you look scared?"

"There are some things we shouldn't speak of. I can't." Her head whipped toward the loft and Tabitha's bedroom.

"Why do you keep lying to me?"

Giada had never been this cryptic about anything before. Over the years, Tabitha had asked many questions, and she'd answered each of them, seemingly with honesty. She talked about her life, her alcoholic father, the child she'd lost, and her abusive husband. Tabitha didn't think there were any secrets between them.

Giada's focus shifted to the archway to Tabitha's left. Ivy had sprouted from a pair of spots on the wall, making a whispering sound as it grew. The ends spiraled lazily down the wall, drawing the wide edges of the frame for the double doors.

Tabitha rose from her stool, placed her brush on the palette. This was different from the previous appearance of the doors, that much she could tell. This time, they didn't struggle for existence. They were making an entrance. Someone was trying to impress her.

As the ivy reached the floor, the doors materialized. And as she approached, they did not shy from her presence. As she reached out to touch them, they swung open inward.

Shielding her eyes from the searing burst of light, she blinked into the brilliance. As it faded, a hallway appeared on the other side of the threshold. She stepped closer to the space that couldn't possibly exist. That wall was at the back of the building, which meant a real door in that place would've led to the back yard and the wooded area behind the church.

"I'm going through," Tabitha said.

Giada shook her head. "What if you can't come back? What if he traps you in there?"

"Who? Orrin?"

"Yes, but he isn't alone. I sense...many."

"Many spirits?"

Giada replied with a nod.

A shrill cry rose from the other side of the door, dancing along every nerve ending in Tabitha's body, raising the hair on her arms. The sound climbed higher until it rang in the rafters like some otherworldly bell. Tabitha covered her ears and closed her eyes, trying to shut out the assault.

Then, as if it finally found the frequency it wanted, the sound morphed into a more familiar one, an earthly one. Somewhere inside the hallway that didn't exist, an infant cried.

"My baby," Giada said as she moved toward the door.

"Wait." Tabitha reached out to catch her, but her hand passed through the green fog of Giada's ghostly arm. "That can't be her."

In life, Giada lost her infant daughter. She hadn't told Tabitha the details, only that the little girl had died in an accident. It was her greatest heartbreak and likely the thing that kept her bound to the world of the living.

Giada broke into a run but vanished from sight before she reached the hallway.

Tabitha's breath hitched in her throat. This didn't make sense. Did Giada vanish because she tried to cross over? If Tabitha tried to cross, would the same thing happen to her?

She stood for a moment, paralyzed by fear and uncertainty. This had to be a trap, but what could the dead really do to the living? If they were like Giada, they had no substance, only presence as something between life and death.

But this. This was nothing like Giada.

It had to be a door to the spirit realm. What happened to the living people who ended up on the wrong side of the veil? Nothing in the many books she'd read on spiritualism and mediumship prepared her for this decision. What else was there for her to do? Cower in fear until it vanished again? What if Giada was in there and needed her?

"Damn," she muttered.

The rug just inside the door matched the rugs that covered the wood floor inside the real church, and it felt just as plush as she stepped onto it. The walls were the same shade of sanctuary white. All in all, the place seemed like an extension of the version in the mortal world, except for the white marble relief that ran along the wall to her right.

It depicted a procession of creatures, human bodies with the heads of beasts, their faces contorted in expressions both alien and terrifying. They moved in a grotesque dance—some twisting in wild, ecstatic movements, others lined up as if for some terrible judgment. The larger ones watched over the smaller ones with a predator's patience, accepting offerings of fruit with a silent, ominous grace.

A whispering came from behind Tabitha. She turned and found a wall of violently green ivy around the door, leaves and stems traveling slowly, creeping across the wooden planks and the red rug, toward her feet.

Tabitha backed away. Her back struck something hard. She wheeled around.

A bare-chested man made of white marble stood there. He towered over her, his head that of a bull.

Her scream refused to come into the world. She turned to run, but more of them had gathered around, a woman with the head of a hare, another with the head of a falcon, all made of marble, all smelling of moss and earth. Their faces were expressionless. Their eyes were blank, statue eyes.

"What..." It was the only word she could pull from the depths of her terror. This couldn't be real.

Spirits closed in around her, clutching at her clothing, pressing her skin with cold, hard flesh. Their breathing was ragged and desperate. If they were spirits, why did they breathe? If not spirits, then what were they?

One of them grabbed the back of her hair, yanking the top of her head backward, sending a shot of pain down her spine. It was the bull man, his mouth inches from her face. His breath was like winter wind against her skin.

"Please," she said. "Don't."

Don't what? Don't hurt me? Don't kill me? Don't stop? This had gone too far, and somehow, not as far as she needed.

"Enough," a deep, male voice commanded from somewhere out of sight, the resonance vibrating through the very marrow of her bones. She knew that sound, recognized the way it tugged at something buried deep within her. Orrin.

The tangle of pale limbs receded. Hands released her. Her scalp ached. Once they were gone, there he stood. As dapper as his photos, wearing that bright, welcoming smile like the world belonged to him, there stood Orrin Riley, wearing a black suit and looking alive and well.

He asked, "Did you get what you came for, Ms. Mainwater?"

No. She had come for him, for this. To be closer to him was to bask in power.

The animal spirits, if that's what they were, retreated to their spots on the wall, returning to their dances and offerings, the same positions as before. And they went still as they did so, the life in them departing as quickly and quietly as it arrived.

She glanced back toward the door that led to the sanctuary. Just as before, it stood open, but on this side, ivy covered the door frame completely. Music from her record player, "Stardust" by Nat King Cole, drifted in, and the song calmed her. She turned back to Orrin.

He bowed at the waist and offered his hand. "Care to dance?"

Despite her longing, she hesitated. Once in his embrace, how well could she resist whatever temptation he presented. Dread never felt so tantalizing, danger so alluring.

"Just a dance, I promise."

She didn't remember taking his hand, but a moment later, his arm was around her, the sedating effect of his touch crowding out all worry. They were no longer in a hallway but on a dance floor, and the music had changed to some kind of waltz that echoed in her mind.

Like the statue people, he smelled of earth, but there was a hint of spiced wine. The smell reminded her of winter and roaring fires and made her feel safe in a place that should have terrified her.

"Where am I?" she asked. "Is this the other side?"

He didn't seem like a spirit, not like Giada. He had substance. He was solid, the fine quality fabric of his suit soft under her fingers. She resisted an urge to lay her head on his shoulder.

"It is the other side of what you believe is possible." He swung them another direction, shifting the waltz away from the door. His smile was reassuring.

She remembered her true purpose. "I'm looking for a friend of mine, who died when we were children."

He laughed. "This is but a small thing. More power than you can imagine dwells within you. We are like gods."

"We?"

"We are the same, you and I. We see things for what they truly are. Evolved spirits offer so much more in the way of spiritual knowledge and ability. All you have to do is give yourself over to me."

The gaze of many pressed against her from all angles. She couldn't see them, of course, but their envy of her with him lingered in the air, oppressive.

She couldn't blame them. He was temptation walking, classically handsome, and the way he carried himself...she'd never seen this kind of ease and grace from a living man.

In a voice that carried more lust than she intended, she asked, "And what exactly would that entail?"

" All that surrounds us is my creation. Here, I am a god. Let me teach you how to move through this realm, how to create from the sliver of divine energy that lives within you."

He looked deep in her eyes, and that scent of spiced wine crashed over her, and she relaxed into the rhythm of the waltz and his energy. *What would kissing him be like?*

He raised an eyebrow as if he sensed her thought. "Tell me your deepest desire."

"To speak with my dead."

"Superficial. Try again. Speak from your soul this time."

She thought for a moment and replied, "Connection."

"There it is. Connection is what we all crave." He put his hand on her cheek, his skin soft and warm, and she leaned into his touch. "Let me teach you." His eyes were lit from within like storm clouds hiding a pale sun. "Accept my influence. Let me in. I will show you everything."

Tabitha reminded herself that this man was a murderer. He was a cult leader. By all accounts, in life, he was nothing to trifle with, but here, all she felt was acceptance, and she couldn't help but gravitate toward it.

"I accept."

A smile curled across his lips, the kind that made her heart flutter in her chest. She swallowed. Without a word, he tilted her chin upward, his fingers cool against her skin.

When his mouth finally descended on hers, sensations clashed within her, a fear of this complete madness, a bottomless sense of need within herself. His lips were firm and insistent, coaxing a moan from her. How she longed to give him everything. In the energy of the moment, two souls joining, she decided she could love him. She would be safe here, as long as she gave him what he wanted.

The light of the hallway faded, and she landed on cold, hard ground. She released the autumn leaves she clutched in her hands.

Ivy tangled her legs as she tried to stand, tried to get her bearings in the darkness. She thrashed until she freed herself and stood on trembling legs, on bare feet.

Tall windows loomed over her, spilling golden light onto the ground. She was behind the church, in the forest, her panicked breath steaming in the frigid air.

A howl came from somewhere nearby, echoing. The sound became a chorus of many that filled the night.

Tabitha ran. She sprinted around the church, fallen sticks and rocks and who knew what else cutting the soles of her feet. Then she was stumbling up the steps, praying the doors were unlocked. Before she could reach them, the doors flew open. And she stumbled into their embrace, into the warmth, back into Orrin's house of miracles.

Chapter 8

The insistent ring of her phone dredged her from the depths of sleep. Instinctively, she reached for her nightstand, fumbling until she found the phone. She answered without looking at the screen.

"Hello?" Her voice sounded dreamy and faraway, even to her.

"Cute, little town, this one." Philip's voice at the other end of the connection snapped her into wakefulness. "Did you know that God commanded the Israelis to destroy the city of Jericho?"

Jericho...the name of the nearest town. He was too close.

"What are you doing?" Tabitha struggled to hold the fear from her voice. That was exactly what he wanted, her fear.

"God said the people of Jericho were evil, but one does have to wonder what version of evil that was. Those wacky followers of His have an interesting idea of right and wrong sometimes, am I right?" Then he laughed.

"Answer me, Philip." Her heart pounded in her chest, each rapid beat sending waves of vertigo through her. To go from sleep to full panic made it hard to think, hard to decide what to do next. She needed to wake the hell up.

"You ask the right people the right questions, they always talk. It's like they never quite know when to shut the fuck up, and that's exactly what I like about them. The only thing left is for me to figure out exactly where your new place is. I'm getting close."

"I'll call the police."

"Why? I haven't done anything to you. Frankly, I don't understand what your problem is. I could've hurt you so much worse. I could've...anyway, I didn't deserve to be abandoned. You could, at least, apologize to me."

It was her turn to laugh. "Apologize? You were controlling." She stood up and felt better with her feet on the floor.

"Someone has to keep you in line. You do your best work that way. Tell me where you are, and I'll show you how rewarding submission can be."

"No."

"I know you remember that night at the hotel in New York, after the art gala."

"Stop."

"You liked that heavy hand guiding you to the elevator, holding you so you didn't stumble, gripping you so you didn't get more than an arm's length from me."

Tabitha did remember that night. She drank too much bourbon. Philip got angry. He didn't hurt her, not much. He'd done a lot of grabbing and a lot of cornering her in spaces, where he got so close that he was all she could see. Alcohol had blurred the edges of the chaos, until the violence felt distant, like something happening through a hazy lens. How she'd laughed. How she'd encouraged him.

She hadn't found the bruises until the next morning. Explanations, excuses, the shame of it all flowed through her as easily as if it belonged there all along, because deep down, she deserved it. The punishment set things right. It restored the equilibrium and made her feel real in the world and alive.

"Stay away from me." She hung up on him and tossed the phone onto the bed.

Tabitha buried her face in her hands and stood that way for a moment, as if she could block out reality. This place should've been safe, tucked away out in the middle of nowhere, nestled among the harvested fields and the forests. The quiet should've insulated her from her past.

This time, when he found her, he'd be worse than ever because she tried to hide from him. She kept things from him. What she needed was a plan.

"A gun." The voice in her mind was Orrin's.

"Giada?" She suddenly remembered her friend's disappearing act from the night before. "Are you here?"

In a swirl of pale, green haze, the ghost appeared at the foot of Tabitha's bed, looking sheepish.

Tabitha sighed with relief. "Are you alright? What happened to you?"

"I don't remember. I'm sorry." The expression on her face was strange, unsettled. Giada was hiding something.

"What do you remember? The last thing, I mean."

"The door."

"You can tell me."

The ghost's expression shifted to one of annoyance. "I am telling you." Her tone hardened in a way Tabitha had never heard.

"Alright. If you want to talk about it, I'm here."

Giada vanished.

"Touchy," Tabitha muttered under her breath and then addressed the seemingly empty room. "Philip might show up. He called this morning. I thought you should know, in case you didn't hear."

Once she made sure the front door was locked, she went about her business, sitting at the desk in the sanctuary, returning phone calls from potential clients. In the afternoon, she turned to painting. The subject was Millicent Holmes, an older woman from the next county over.

After stopping her heart medication a couple of months prior, she'd died in her sleep. Her family wanted her portrait to feature a younger version of Millicent, maybe because that was the version of her that hadn't yet grown tired of living. Tabitha respected her decision to go out on her own terms.

In her youth, Millicent was a raven-haired beauty with a face like a classic movie star. The photograph had ignited a creative spark in Tabitha like nothing had in a while. As the portrait progressed, it had taken on a life of its own, calling for colors and composition she didn't ordinarily use. Part of her hoped the family would reject the painting altogether so she could keep it for her own. She would gladly refund their money.

Her phone remained ominously silent as she worked, sitting on the table next to her. He was getting closer. Otherwise, he'd be calling to harass her or demand more answers. What if he already had her address? How far would he go once he got there?

He'd never hurt her before, not in a way that anyone would see as significant. The cops probably wouldn't even take her seriously if she called, unless she was in imminent danger, and then? Then she would just have to hope they got there in time before Philip did any real damage.

Maybe part of her didn't want them to come.

"A gun." Orrin spoke again from somewhere deep within her, his words more insistent. Was he really speaking to her or had her mind just latched onto the smooth, even tone of his voice?

"Where?" she asked aloud.

The voice of Orrin did not reply.

Sunset painted the sanctuary walls in shades of flame. As the fire dimmed, anxiety bloomed somewhere deep within her, the energy of it dancing along her nerves. If she wanted to get through this, she had to channel it into anger. Even if he wasn't really coming, she had to be ready.

She put Billie Holiday's "All or Nothing at All" on the record player to soothe her nerves. Jazz music pushed back the heavy silence, Holiday's voice drifting lazily, forcing normalcy into a place that had known no such thing.

Tabitha paced. She made slow laps through the sanctuary, occasionally removing items from the last few boxes she hadn't unpacked and arranging them on shelves or placing them in drawers. All the while, the largest knife from her kitchen drawer kept her company. She carried it with her, placing it on whatever surface was closest when she found something new to occupy her restless mind.

Night descended quickly and silently, blanketing the church with the same wet earth scent of the previous night. She had hoped that if Philip was going to appear, he would do it while the sun was still up. What was he waiting for?

Now, instead of one man, she felt the approach of two. Orrin would return, and she wanted him to. Could he protect her from Philip?

"Orrin?" She called his name from the center of the sanctuary, turning in a slow circle as if he might emerge from any corner, any wall.

The door appeared just as it had the previous night, more quickly this time as if it had gained strength, and she let a gasp of relief. She wouldn't have to face this alone, after all. She wasn't sure he could do anything but scare her ex off, but maybe that would be enough.

He flung the double doors wide, stepping into the sanctuary as though he still ruled it, every inch of him dripping with effortless authority. The black suit clung to him like a shadow, his slicked-back hair gleaming under the dim light. He moved with the grace of a god, pausing only when he stood before Tabitha. He extended a hand, a silent command wrapped in the guise of an invitation.

She hesitated but accepted, her fingers slipping into his, and the moment their skin touched, music rose from the corners of the room, a haunting melody that drowned out the music from her record player and wrapped itself around them. His power surged through her, sending a shiver down her spine. The waltz he led was precise, almost too perfect, yet tinged with an unsettling edge, as if some unseen force threatened to pull her under. She struggled to keep pace, nearly stumbling as they spun, gravity bending beneath the weight of his presence.

His voice was low and sultry. "You've allowed rage to sit in your heart for so long, you no longer feel the fire of it."

"A man is coming here. I'm afraid he'll hurt me."

"He cannot possibly harm you, not if you welcome the power that already lives within you." He smiled, then, as if he'd just shared the secret to everything.

"Tell me," she said as the sanctuary vanished in a blur of motion and music.

"I have a gift for you, but you'll have to earn it, first."

"I don't want to play games anymore."

"But I adore the games. They make rewards all the sweeter."

"I prefer answers."

"Then answers you shall have, sweet Tabitha." He stopped their dance, but the sanctuary kept spinning and tilting on its axis. "I want you to feel the pulse of the earth."

She wanted to feel nothing more than his arms around her. There, she was safe. There, he could whisper dreams to her all night, for the rest of eternity if he liked. All he had to do was ask.

"How?"

"Close your eyes and breathe."

She did as he asked.

"Picture this man, who is foolish enough to come for you."

Philip. At first, in her mind, it was the night he caught her flirting with another man. They were at a bar. The flirting was innocent enough, a few words exchanged when she went to the bar for another drink. She'd gotten caught up in the thundering boom of the music and the sense of freedom. But Philip was standing behind her, and when he saw her speak to another man, he'd yanked her away, back into the crowd, where he berated under flashing lights.

The scene unraveled, slipping away like a wisp of smoke, only to reveal a new one. She was alone on a dark, country road, surrounded by farm fields. A deep voice rumbled in her throat, muttering words she hadn't summoned. She recognized it immediately. Somehow, she had become a passenger behind Philip's eyes as he walked along in the dark, his bare feet cold on the ground.

She said, "I don't understand."

"More. Dig in," Orrin urged.

She reached further and heard the dull thud of his heart, felt the scrambled state of his mind. He didn't know where he was.

"Did you do this?" Tabitha asked Orrin.

She was, somehow, in two places at once, careening between her own body and Philip's perspective, the sensations of two beings at once pushing her toward the brink of overload.

Orrin didn't reply.

Blood trickled down Philip's arm, an injury to his shoulder. His left eye throbbed, and she couldn't see from it. She touched it with one cold hand and felt how swollen it was.

"I'm going fucking kill you," Philip said as he continued to plod along.

Tabitha said to Orrin, "Tell me what this is."

He tightened his grip on her and leaned in to whisper into her ear, "It is a hunt."

"I can't do this." She tried to pull away but couldn't.

He cradled her face in one hand, and she leaned into his touch, unable to resist. "Be what you are. It's so easy when you know what comes after. There is no end. There is only riddance of foul energy. This life can be whatever you desire. You need only feed the part of you that wants."

"I don't want this."

The waltz started once more.

Orrin asked, "What do you think he intends to do when he gets here? Will he reconcile? Will he be reasonable? Tell me what you believe his intentions are."

"He's coming here to hurt me."

"Good girl. We all know what vile pigs men can be."

Deep in the dark cold, Philip kept walking. He turned at the corner, a half-mile down the road from Lucas' farm. With dainty fangs, the cold bit his skin, giving rise to goose flesh.

Orrin said, "Find your rage again. What does it say to you?"

"No."

"Yes." Orrin spoke through clenched teeth. "If you could do anything to that man with no consequences...dream it for me."

"No."

He curled a finger under her chin, tipped her face up, met her gaze, and said, "Let go. Let it burn."

His lips found hers, and the fire surged through her, a hunger she had never known flaring to life. The flames inside her clawed upward, threatening to consume. She pushed away from him, and that time, he released her.

Fists clenched, she roared, rage burning along every inch of her skin, and all of a sudden, she couldn't wait for Philip to see what she had become. She turned to Orrin.

"The gun. Where is it?"

A smile crept across his face. "Your reward is in the basement."

Tabitha broke into a run. Philip was close, too close, turning onto the gravel driveway. His pain was significant, but it would be over soon.

She threw open the door, nearly tumbled down the basement stairs in her desperation. Orrin waited for her at the bottom. He pointed to the edge of the room, at a bundle of ivy she hadn't noticed before. She went to her knees, plunged her hands into the tangle of leaves and stems.

The rifle she pulled out was heavy and old. Tabitha had never shot a gun before, but this sensation, the balance of the thing, was somehow familiar. She cocked it. How did she know how to do it? Why did this feel so natural?

Orrin spoke from behind her. "It is the power that feels familiar. It has always lived within you. Let me help."

She stood and faced him.

"Do you feel the pulse of the earth yet? Have you chosen your spirit?"

She thought for a moment. "The animal spirits from the behind the door."

"Yes. The ancients knew the importance of channeling the energy of the natural world. When we embody our natures, we harness our highest power. Close your eyes and try."

Tabitha did as he said, felt her feet on the cold floor, felt her spirit reach through the concrete. Beneath the man-made, within the earth, a fire burned, shadows moving within. The largest of them, a creature wearing the antlers of a great stag, loomed over the flames, his skin a bottomless void, his blood made of smoke from the gnarled bodies burning at his feet.

With a clawed hand, it reached for her, gripped her heart, and squeezed until the pain blinded her in a flash of white. Gone was the floor beneath her feet. Orrin was miles away. No one would save her from this.

"Please," she said with the only breath she could muster.

"I am the beginning and the end, the ancient that stirs in the dark. Devote yourself to me." The baritone voice cut through the agony and the blindness. It became her world.

The grip around her heart tightened. Somewhere far away, her body shuddered, and the rifle clattered across the basement floor. A vision of herself entered her consciousness, face tipped toward the ceiling, eyes wide and dark with specks of stars dancing through the inky blackness. Orrin held up her limp form, whispering words she couldn't understand. He had betrayed her.

The church doorbell rang.

"Release me," she said.

"Worship me."

"No."

The shadowy form opened its mouth, revealing the raw, red power fueling it. The roar it released ripped through her soul, and both worlds spun away.

Orrin's calm voice reached her. "He's at your door, darling. You'd better go."

Before she realized she was conscious, she was stumbling down the hallway, making her way from the basement to the front door, the red rug grabbing at her bare feet and rising and falling like an ocean. Walls seemed to bend under her touch. The rifle in her hand was the only thing that felt solid, and she anchored herself to it.

The knock at the door was relentless. It hounded her from the moment she heard it until she grabbed the handle and pulled one of the doors open to the night.

There he was. The mortal man she feared stood on the stairs outside, looking disoriented and angry. He swayed on his feet almost as much as she did.

"Let me in," Philip said, and then he laughed. "How did I get here? Where am I?"

And the rage that lived in her for so long flared. The cruel words he'd spoken to her during the course of their three-year relationship played like chorus in her mind, claims that she was nothing without him, that she couldn't take care of herself, that she was broken, and he was the only one who could fix her. Didn't she appreciate everything he'd done for her?

Tabitha leveled rifle.

"Wait." He put up his hands.

She pulled the trigger.

Chapter 9

Tabitha dreamed.

She dreamed of ivy dragging a corpse toward the spirit door at the front of the sanctuary.

She dreamed of blood and the gaping hole in Philip's forehead.

She dreamed of the way the shot echoed in the dark forest.

Demon...that was the name for the creature she met. Once her mind had time to find its footing, it presented her with this unwelcome realization.

Tabitha was lying on her back, on the floor of the sanctuary, her head in Orrin's lap as he sat on the floor with her. Quiet jazz drifted from her record player in the corner. An icy breeze from the open front door had failed to dissipate the stench of gunpowder. It was all she could smell, that and the blood.

"My lioness," Orrin said as he stroked her hair. "Despite your best efforts, you found your way."

She jolted upright, stood on trembling legs. "What did you do?"

"What did I do?" He rose with her, incredulous, one hand on his chest to feign innocence.

Tabitha's hand cooled her forehead. "Was it real?"

"Reality is always a matter of perspective, isn't it?" She barely heard his honey voice over the panic rushing through her veins.

"Where is the body?"

"I've taken care of the remains, if that's what you're worried about."

"I want to see it."

"Now, why would you want a thing so morbid? Gentle souls such as yours should be protected from the likes."

"I need to know for sure."

"You already know."

"I don't, though." She wheeled around, stepped toward the door but then turned to look in the direction of the basement. If she could just get her bearings, figure out where she lost track of herself. She asked, "Where's the gun?"

"You don't need it anymore." Orrin rested his hand on the small of her back, his touch soothing, but that was how he wanted her to feel.

"Why won't you tell me anything?"

"Come here." He curled a finger under her chin, a quiet demand for her to shift her gaze to his. "While you're under my protection, you need not worry. No man will harm you."

They'd moved, somehow, and now stood at the center of the sanctuary, in front of the door that led to his world. The church front door still stood open, a gaping hole allowing the night chill to cavort through the sanctuary. She shivered.

"I want answers," she said in a voice that was weaker than she wanted. "I—I don't understand...any of this."

"You will understand in time; I promise you that. Until then, I need you to trust me. Do you trust me?"

She considered all that had happened, the demon, her helplessness under the supernatural influence, and she said, "I don't." And then she stepped back. "If you want to earn my trust, take me to Philip."

At first, he let her go, but only to ensnare her once more in his grasp, their dance shifting yet again. The kitchen island's unforgiving edge became his accomplice as he pinned her against it. His hand was on her throat, his face so close to hers that she could no longer make out his features.

"Understand that you are mine." There was no more honey in his voice. His grip tightened, and he pressed in.

When Tabitha was still with Philip, on the nights when the drama really went off the deep end, a switch somewhere deep within the recesses of her mind would flip, and his assaults, which should've scared her, triggered submission within her. Those were the nights she surrendered to whatever he wanted. And the next morning, she would hate herself for not fighting back more.

Her disgust with herself ran deep, because on some level, she got off on being treated like she deserved it. Otherwise, she would've left him sooner. She would've called the police. Instead, for too long, she kept loving him in ways he didn't deserve.

Now, Orrin triggered that unnatural sense of calm, like a piece of the puzzle finding its place in her troubled mind. Her pulse slowed. Her breath found its rhythm once more.

He seemed to sense this shift and backed off as if to get a better look at her. His eyes narrowed in an expression that was a mix of confusion and suspicion.

Tires crunched on gravel outside, a car pulling into the driveway.

Tabitha left Orrin for the front door, shielding her eyes from headlights as she reached the threshold. Moments passed like hours in the blinding light as her mind reeled with possibilities. Who was there? Cops? Maybe Philip himself, alive and well and ready to bring the full brunt of his anger. She might welcome that at this point. At least, it would mean that she wasn't a murderer.

The driver cut the engine, and the vehicle door opened and closed, and fear surged within her.

"Ms. Mainwater?" Lucas called out from next to his truck. "Are you alright? I thought I heard a gunshot."

"No gunshot here. I'm fine."

"What happened?" Then he was at the top of the steps.

Could he smell the gunpowder? Could he smell the blood? He didn't seem like he did.

"I don't know."

What to tell him? She wasn't even sure what was real and what wasn't. Before she talked to anyone, she needed time to figure out where she was and who she'd been. Too quickly, she was losing track.

"What happened to your arm?" he asked.

She followed his gaze to her left forearm, where three scratches ran from her elbow to just above her wrist. They weren't bleeding, but they were angry, and now that she noticed them, they felt hot. She offered the first explanation that came to mind.

"I think I fell."

"Maybe we should get you to a hospital."

"No," she said with more force than she intended. "I just woke up. I'm okay. Scout's honor." She offered a reassuring smile.

His doubt evident, he nodded anyway. "Alright. Well, I'm here if you need me."

Jackal sniffed intently at the concrete at Lucas' feet, the spot where Philip was standing when Tabitha shot him.

There was no blood, no evidence that he was there at all.

"Thanks. I appreciate you checking on me. If you don't mind, I'm going to get back to my painting." She moved to close the double doors. "Have a nice evening. Bye, Jackal."

Once the doors were closed, she leaned against them, listened as Lucas reversed the old truck out of her driveway.

When she turned, Orrin was gone. The spirit door was gone, too.

Too close. Everything was too close. Moments constricted around her, suffocating in the way they collided and blurred. She needed to find reality. She needed to land somewhere solid, so she could formulate a plan to get what she wanted. The idea of finding Rebecca's spirit still lived in the forefront of her thoughts, but did she want the child's spirit mixed up in whatever this was?

No.

She'd have to use Orrin and his demon (if that's what it was) to learn how to navigate the spirit plane and then leave them both behind. This plan was dangerous. They wouldn't let her go, not by choice.

They might not even let her live. She needed to know what their end game was, and then she could dangle it in front of them to get what she wanted.

"Giada." Tabitha spoke aloud, not a request but a demand. When the ghost did not appear, she tried again, this time fueling the demand with the anger she felt at being abandoned by someone who claimed to be her friend. "Giada."

At last, she did appear in a swirl of pale, green vapor, stumbling a little as if nudged by someone or something. She looked around for a moment, confused.

"How did you do that?"

"Where have you been?"

"I don't know."

"Stop lying to me."

"Mr. Riley...he puts me in a room. Sometimes, I hear voices." She touched her face and then her hair. "They terrify me, but I don't want to leave. My baby could be there."

"Your baby is not there. You know she isn't." The words felt cruel but necessary. Tabitha needed Giada with her and on her side.

"She might be." The ghost's voice was weaker.

Tabitha met her gaze. "You're going to stay with me, and you're going to focus. Am I clear?"

Giada's expression faltered. "I don't have to."

"Yes, you do. Tell me you will."

"But I always have a choice."

"Not this time."

Giada faded from view.

Tabitha didn't know what came over her, but she raised a hand and snapped her fingers. The ghost reappeared, looking hurt, like a wild animal realizing it had been cornered.

"Not this time." Tabitha repeated the words.

Chapter 10

"God damn it, Tabitha. If you'd just listen to me, do what I tell you, everything could be perfect. But instead, you run around acting like I don't matter." Philip's voice echoed through her thoughts.

Did she really kill him? The question played over and over in her mind the next morning as she struggled to paint Millicent. It could've been a dream or some sort of hallucination.

As she sat in the sanctuary, putting brush to canvas, her phone remained quiet on the table next to her, the screen dark as night.

Philip didn't deserve to die, did he? Maybe that depended on his intentions. But what intentions could a man wandering barefoot down a country road have? If he were real, he wasn't in control; that much she knew, and that much made the whole situation worse.

In the early afternoon, after staring at Millicent's classic movie star smile for too long, she put the painting aside and pulled out a fresh canvas.

Lioness. That's what Orrin had called her. She imagined herself as one of the animal spirits in Orrin's realm, the ones made of white marble, and then she began sketching.

His lioness, that's what he'd called her.

His as if he already owned her.

No.

Tabitha threw the pencil across the room. She couldn't let herself be a victim again.

She paced around the sanctuary for a while, grappling with her conscience, arguing with herself about whether she'd actually killed Philip, until she finally snatched up the phone.

One ring, two rings, three. Voicemail.

The dead man's voice rang in her ears, but her pulse was by far the loudest sound in the room. No way he would've missed an opportunity to answer a call from her. He should've answered. He should've bragged about how close he was to finding her.

Too late, Tabitha realized she'd gnawed one of her fingernails bloody.

"Shit."

She'd picked up the habit after Rebecca died. It was mostly subconscious, happening when she was stressed. But there were times she'd done it out of anger. Extreme nail-biting was always a surefire way to get her parents' attention. All she had to do was draw a little blood...

Cold water from the kitchen faucet cooled the bite of pain, and the swirl of blood down the drain felt like some strange offering to the church.

Once again, Orrin crept into her thoughts, insidious as a shadow slipping through a crack, the memory of his hand tightening around her throat sending a spark of heat racing through her. He offered power, and it was probably power she could use, but how?

When Orrin ran his Church of Ascendants, he taught people that death would make them powerful, that once they'd achieved his version of enlightenment on this plane, they'd be allowed to move on. They would be gods. They likely drew at least some of that power from Cernunnos.

The box on the counter, the one containing his writings, drew her to it once more. She'd already dug through the thing, but now she knew more. Now she might notice something she previously overlooked, because now her soul was in more danger than ever before.

Tabitha went through the journals again, page by page, word by word, searching for the meaning behind the meaning. She spread the notes out across the counter, trying to piece them together in some new way.

There were numbers and calendars, lines and arrows linking ideas that floated in the margins, geometric shapes that signified...something. At the center of the mess, she'd placed a sketch of antlers. These represented Cernunnos, the creature she'd seen looming over a pile of burning bodies. If she wanted to leverage her connection to the spirit world, she needed to understand exactly what she was dealing with.

Orrin was one thing, but this...this was the real power, the way Cernunnos had so completely overwhelmed her. Had he taken something from her or given her something? There was a gift in the darkness; she was sure, but that gift would have a price.

There was one person she trusted enough to ask for help. She picked up the phone.

Chapter 11

The autumn day was bright as Tabitha drove to downtown Jericho, on her way to Stellar Café to meet with her mentor, Constance Valentine Deschane.

The café, situated at the bustling corner of Main Street and White Oak, was a tiny, brick place with a black wrought iron fence around the outdoor dining area. Tabitha found sixty-year-old Constance sitting at a table there, clad in her usual mismatched animal prints and glittery horn-rimmed glasses, sipping iced tea. Her dark hair was grayer and shorter than the last time they'd met a few years prior.

"Thank you for coming." Tabitha took a seat across the table.

Unsmiling, Constance said in her mid-Atlantic accent, "Dahling, if anyone else tried to summon me to this hellhole of a town, I would've told them to take a flying leap into a sea of rabid otters."

"I didn't think—"

"As per usual. You didn't think when you abandoned your training. You didn't think when you bought that vortex of evil."

"You heard about that?"

"Of course, I did. It is good to see you, even under these circumstances." Constance reached out and touched Tabitha's hand. "Go on and tell Auntie what you're dealing with."

Tabitha gave her the full rundown about Orrin, the door, the animal-headed spirits, and Cernunnos. She omitted the incident with Philip in case what she'd experienced was real. The last thing she needed was a murder charge.

"Where is Giada in all this?"

"What?" Tabitha hadn't expected her to come up in conversation.

Constance never approved of their friendship. She believed that safety was paramount, and to maintain that safety, one should never get too close to the spirit world.

"I don't sense her presence. Where is she?"

"Do you want me to call for her?"

"Good lord. Not here." Constance sighed. "I wanted to ask her thoughts. I was hoping for another perspective. You seem too tangled up in this nonsense. I can see it in your eyes. You aren't ready for this level of spiritual involvement." She let an incredulous burst of laughter. "Hell, I'm not ready for this level."

"What I really need is information about Cernunnos. Every time I try to look up the name on my phone or the internet, my browser stops functioning."

"And you, of all people, should know what that is."

"Interference."

"Yes, dear, and it's likely your new ghostly boyfriend providing that interference."

"Not boyfriend."

"Liar. Do you think you'd be the first medium to become romantically entangled with a spirit? You probably wouldn't be the first one this month. The dead were once living. Therefore, they know what the living want, and how to make vulnerable people enact their wishes on the mortal plane."

"Why are you being condescending? I'm not your student anymore."

"Why are you being defensive? I merely stated a fact. What has he offered that you want or need?"

Power. Philip gone. And she had to admit to herself that her attraction to him was...intense.

"I need information about Cernunnos."

Constance narrowed her eyes. "Why?"

"I need to hold him at bay while I learn what I can from Orrin."

"What you *need* to leave that church behind. It's too dangerous."

"That's for me to decide."

"You don't get to decide what is or isn't dangerous."

"No, but I do get to choose what danger is worth facing. You know I've struggled to make contact with spirits other than Giada. This could be my only chance."

"As I have explained to you so many times before, the solution to that problem is patience and time, not tossing yourself into a pit of poltergeists."

"I'm not leaving. You can either help me protect myself or abandon me."

Constance rolled her eyes. "Your Cernunnos is a Pagan god of life and death. In Christianity, his appearance is sometimes used to represent the antichrist. Does that sound like an entity that a medium of somewhat questionable skill should be dancing around?"

It sounded like a being that could grant immense power.

"I'll be fine."

Constance shook her head. "Arrogance. Nothing has changed."

"Stubbornness. Nothing has changed."

Constance barked out a laugh.

Tabitha said, "I need to do this. Please help me."

She studied Tabitha for several seconds while a cold, autumn breeze ruffled her salt-and-pepper hair. "Orrin and Cernunnos have no intention of offering you power. If anything, they want to steal it from you."

"I know."

"Then why go on? Why not escape while you can?"

"I'm trying to be careful. That's why I called you."

"There is no 'careful' in this predicament."

"I understand."

With a disgusted expression on her face, Constance reached up to her neck to unclasp a necklace and dropped it onto the table. "It's a cross of St. Benedict, protection against evil and curses."

The round medallion was silver and warm in Tabitha's hand, its surface bearing the weight of centuries-old devotion. Etched at its center, a Latin cross was surrounded by cryptic inscriptions. On the other side, the saint himself stood before what looked like an altar. If nothing else, Catholics excelled at spiritual trinkets.

"Thank you."

"You know the other options. Incense and sage for cleansing. Salt."

"I don't want to get rid of them."

"You probably couldn't if you wanted to, dear. No offense." Constance's tone had turned somber.

"None taken."

A heavy sensation sank into the depths of Tabitha's stomach. She'd known the church was dangerous before she even saw it, but the gravity of the situation now bore down on her with fresh intensity. This could be goodbye. Or maybe it felt that way to Constance, and Tabitha just sensed the energy.

"If you insist on going through Orrin's door, what you really need is an anchor to the mortal plane. Otherwise, he could trap you there."

"What kind of anchor?"

"Only you can decide what keeps you on this side of the veil." She got up to leave, and Tabitha stood with her.

"That's it?"

"I've given you what I have to offer, the most important part being that I tried to discourage you from going any further. I did my job. Be careful." Then, for the first time in the history of their relationship, Constance hugged her.

Tabitha stood in the middle of the café dining area, watching Constance go, wondering if this would be the last time. She breathed in the cool air, listened to the sounds of birds and the murmur of conversation around her.

No. She wasn't ready to leave this life, not yet. As much as she longed to see Rebecca and her father once more, she had to hold on. Death was not the way.

Tabitha put on the cross.

Chapter 12

Tabitha contemplated the enormous oil portrait of Rebecca hanging on the wall. The visage of the little girl, whose death started it all, looked back, smiling innocently. This version of her had more dramatic flourish than the memory of her that was lodged in Tabitha's mind.

Her dark hair was in ringlets. Her pale skin shone, ethereally iridescent. Her wings were purest white, of course, folded around her as if embracing her small frame. The background was simple, a traditional one that faded to a rich dark brown at the edges, as if her mere presence could push back shadows.

This was Tabitha's anchor to the mortal plane and her purpose.

Giada appeared next to Tabitha in a burst of cool air. Obviously still wary after their previous interaction, she kept her distance.

"I'm sorry," Tabitha said, and she meant it.

"It's alright."

"No, it isn't. I shouldn't have tried to control you."

"Frustration got the better of you is all." Giada hugged herself as if she felt the chill she'd brought in with her. "Do you hear my baby? I hear her all the time now. I think she's...I think she's punishing me."

"Why would your daughter punish you?"

Giada paused. She made a little choking sound and then shook her head as if the words had lodged themselves in her throat.

"We don't have to talk about it."

Giada gave a grateful nod.

Tabitha changed the subject. "I don't know if I'm going to come out of this thing with my soul intact."

"Don't say that."

"No, no. It's okay. I just want you to know that I appreciate our friendship. You've been there for me a lot, more than any living person has. You've tried to help me find Rebecca."

"Loss is an awful thing."

"Like some insurmountable hill I kept trying to climb. Coming here was the only way to make progress. She's over there somewhere; I know it."

"I hope she's worth the price."

The air in the sanctuary grew thick and heavy.

"He's coming," Giada said. Her gaze shifted to the floor, and a lost look came over her.

"Giada?"

She looked up suddenly. "My baby. I hear her. Do you know where she is?" Her eyes darted around the sanctuary, shifting direction, trying to follow the source of the sound from corner to corner.

In the place where the door would appear, a sprig of ivy curled through the plaster wall, crawling and spreading, whispering across every surface it touched. And when the patch of greenery gained enough substance, the white door appeared and cracked open slowly, its light spilling across the plush, red rug.

"She's inside." Giada stumbled in her haste to get through, to enter Orrin's realm.

"Wait!" Tabitha went after her, into the hallway, where she'd seen the animal-headed spirits. They remained in relief form on the wall, motionless, but Tabitha had no doubt they were watching. She felt them as certainly as she felt the shift in gravity and the stifling, earthy air of the hallway.

"Giada!" Tabitha called out.

No answer.

Ahead of her was a junction in the hallway that offered paths to the left and the right. She started toward it, but Orrin appeared in front of her, blocking her path. She staggered back.

"Oh, no. I'm so sorry, beautiful girl." He grinned devilishly. "Now, just where do you think you're going in such a rush?"

"Why are you tormenting Giada?"

"Giada torments herself. The echoes she hears are those of her own grief and shame."

"Why shame?"

He shrugged. "Does it matter? We're all ashamed of something, aren't we?" He stepped closer, took the St. Benedict medallion in his hand to get a closer look at it, and he smelled of musk and spice, strangely comforting in a confining sort of way. It coiled around her, so that he was all she could breathe. "I didn't take you for a Catholic."

"I'm not." Her skin grazed his as she gently plucked it from his fingers to let it lie back on her chest, and she hated the rush of attraction she felt at the contact. She needed to focus. "Tell me about Cernunnos. What does he want from me?"

"Walk with me." In the dim corridor, he moved with a quiet purpose, his figure cutting through the shadows cast by the delicate potted trees that lined the walls like sentinels. The animal spirits etched into the stone seemed to lie in wait, their eyes following them in a way that made the hair at the nape of her neck stand on end. He made a left at the next corner. "Cernunnos wants the same thing I do: your devotion."

"Why?"

Instead of answering, he wheeled back around to face her, looping an arm around her waist and pulling her into a waltz. Music accompaniment, violin and piano, filled the hall with sound and a rhythm she couldn't help but follow. Orrin controlled everything here. He was showing her what she could have if she relinquished control, let herself float along in the romance of the thing.

Their waltz ended at a second door. This one was deep brown, almost black wood, the surface gnarled and wild with leafy branches sprouting from it. He turned from her to place his hand on the wall, bowing his head as if concentrating.

"Answer me," she insisted.

"Because a soul is pure light, and your light burns brighter than most. Were you aware?" He glanced back over his shoulder and caught her gaze with bottomless blue eyes.

He heaved the door open, its hinges letting an otherworldly groan, and a wave of floral-scented air crashed over her. Sunlight poured in, and she squinted. He took her by the hand and then led her through the door.

"I want you to see the beauty of this place. The mortal world pales in comparison."

Beyond the threshold, a garden spread before them, lush beyond lush, with flowering bushes that threatened to overtake the edges of a stone path. Fountains gurgled. Statues were scattered throughout, more of the marble spirits that came to life as Orrin and Tabitha passed through.

They followed, each hoof and claw nearly silent on the stone. Their presence was unnerving, too close to stalking for Tabitha's taste. She tried to ignore them.

She asked, "Do you work for him?"

"I work *with* him. I am not an employee. Big difference."

"Is he here?"

"No. He is on a different plane." Orrin started to sound annoyed, but his patience hadn't yet run out.

"You offered your followers power. This," she motioned to the animal spirits behind them, "doesn't look like power. Is this what you and Cernunnos want for me? To turn me into one of these things?"

Orrin let go of her hand. "These things? These 'things' are beautiful and powerful beyond anything the mortal world had to offer. They chose this version of existence. There is power in peace and beauty." He motioned to one of the spirits, a woman with the head of a rabbit, and she trotted over, eager for the attention. He said, "Show her your power."

The rabbit woman turned to the patch of flowers behind her, waving her bare arms and hands, the human fingers working through the air. A sapling sprouted from the ground, taller and taller, and the trunk widened. Branches spread over their heads, quickly bowing under the weight of ripe, dark plums.

Tabitha picked a plum and bit into it. She'd never tasted anything so sweet and perfect.

She said, "Fantastic. Now, show me something more."

Tabitha needed to get a feel for what they were truly capable of. She needed to know the possibilities, theirs and hers. This display, while beautiful, wouldn't help her.

Orrin chuckled. "I appreciate a woman, who isn't easily impressed. What would impress you, Ms. Mainwater?" He nodded, a gesture for the rabbit woman to make herself scarce, and she slunk off, disappointed with Tabitha's lack of enthusiasm for her work.

"Something bigger than a tree."

"Very well. Close your eyes and take my hand."

Tabitha did as he asked.

Chapter 13

The smell of saltwater reached Tabitha before she opened her eyes. It mingled with the cries of seagulls and the crash of waves against the shore. A sense of wellbeing and safety edged all memory of the danger from her mind. Jewel-toned fabrics cascaded from ceiling to floor, adorned with golden strings of beads, and the rug beneath her feet was ornate and plush.

At the far edge of the room, the wall was open to a cloudless, blue sky. Tabitha released Orrin's hand, drawn to it.

"This is an illusion, yes?"

"All perception is illusion dreamt by each soul, different for each soul." He thought for a moment and added, "You can have whatever you want, even me."

Did he mean romantically? In the not-so-distant past, she would've leapt at the opportunity to have him as her own. To surrender might've been ecstasy. But that was before.

On the wide, stone balcony, high above the surface of the water, the sun kissed her skin with warmth. Gilded torches burned at the corners of the balcony railing. This place—so flawless, so meticulously designed—felt like a dream, or perhaps something more artificial.

"Where are we?" she asked as he joined her.

"The edge of the Mediterranean. Southern France. I was here once with a friend of mine. This place has lived in my mind ever since."

"Is all your power based in illusion?"

"What would you prefer, Ms. Mainwater? Destruction?"

"I don't know. Maybe. This all feels…superficial." She remembered her true purpose. "I want you to teach me how to find people I've lost to death."

"That may take some time."

"What about Cernunnos? Can I ask him to find her?"

"Cernunnos is a god."

"What is a god that refuses to hear the prayers of their followers?"

Orrin stepped closer to her, close enough to move a strand of hair from her face. His eyes were the same shade as the boundless sky.

In a low, soothing voice, he said, "All things in time." And then his arms were around her. His mouth captured hers in a kiss that demanded too much all at once, and she tumbled into it with reckless abandon.

The idea that she shouldn't enjoy kissing a dead man this much crept into her mind, unwelcome. Constance had warned her about such things. They endangered both the life and the soul, but God, how Tabitha loved teetering on this edge. There was something liberating in the action, as if she'd tossed off the shackles that held her to the world of the living.

Orrin finally pulled away, leaving her breathless in his arms. "Rule this realm with me." His tone was that of soft demand. "All we have to do is help Cernunnos reach the mortal plane."

She found her feet and turned to look out over the sea once more. It spanned before her, shining in the light of a sun that only existed here.

She made a demand of her own. "Teach me to do what you do."

"I thought you weren't impressed by illusion."

"It's not illusion, though, is it? Not completely."

"I prefer to think of it as a conjured reality. Here, I can affect anything and everything. I decide what happens here. We decide what is."

He stretched a hand toward the ocean, palm up, and waited. The world went quiet for what felt like a long time, and the air shifted.

Seagulls erupted from below the balcony, flying up and then out, spiraling higher and higher until they were no longer visible. Then gradually, like drops of melancholy, their spectral shapes descended once more, plunging into the saltwater with soft splashes.

"Are they dead?" Tabitha asked.

"Do you think they were alive? Perhaps you could conjure one, and see if it has a pulse."

"I'd rather not play with lives."

"Very well. Try the wind. Create a breeze."

"How?"

"Draw on the energy around you and from the center of your being. The soul is a well. Envision the breeze blowing through tree branches."

She gripped the cross at her throat, the cool metal pressing into her palm as she closed her eyes. Her breath slowed, and she sank deep into herself, searching for the familiar hum in the air, the same crackling charge she always felt around Orrin. As she located her center, Orrin laid a hand on her lower back, encouraging her.

He said, "You can do this, my lioness." Kisses traveling along the back of her neck distracted her for a moment, but she found what she needed.

The breeze started small, swirling across the balcony from her left, sweeping up her long hair. Encouraged, she pushed harder, coaxing the breeze into a gust, its ferocity threatening to wrench her and Orrin from the balcony and toss them mercilessly into the waves below.

"Stop!" Orrin's voice reached her through the roar, but she couldn't do what he wanted. *This* was true power. The sky darkened. The hair at the nape of her neck rose.

The torch at the left corner of the balcony wavered, defiant in the onslaught. She willed the flame higher, and it gleefully complied. Tongues of fire reached out like curious tendrils, exploring the boundaries of their existence until the heat threatened to sear her skin.

"Enough!" Orrin shouted.

Tabitha was suddenly submerged, unable to breath, unable to move, enveloped and suffocating. As darkness threatened to consume her, powerful hands seized her, yanking her upward into the blinding embrace of sunlight. Gasping for breath, she found Orrin holding her by the front of her shirt. They were no longer on the balcony but in the sea, near the shore.

"I said that was enough." Fury had replaced the honeyed tone of his voice. He dragged her to the beach, dropping her roughly onto the sand.

"Sorry," she said once she could breathe.

"This is my world. The only soul allowed to burn it is me." He jabbed fingers into his chest. "If you cannot understand that, we'll have to come up with a better solution."

She gathered strength, hauling herself up to stand and face him. "Am I not free to do as I please?"

"Within *limits*, Ms. Mainwater. I don't want to have to confine you."

A burst of laughter escaped her, but she said nothing. They stared at one another, processing these new shifts in their dynamic: her defiance and his willingness to make her a prisoner.

Finally, he said, "I think it's time for you to go home."

Her mind reeled with possibilities. She had drawn on the power of souls, hers, maybe Orrin's himself. In the rush of adrenaline these realizations brought, another idea sprang to mind. What if she could draw on the power of Cernunnos? Did he have a soul? With that kind of power, she could do more. She could travel beyond this plane.

She said, "Take me to Cernunnos."

"No. Your behavior is already out of hand. I show you miracles, and you choose destruction. Cernunnos doesn't have my patience. He will destroy you."

"You said he needs me."

"We can find another."

Anger simmered within Tabitha. He built her up, only to break her down at the first sign of resistance. Orrin was just like Philip. He wanted control over her, nothing more. Men wanted powerful women until that power posed a threat to their own significance.

Tabitha put her back to Orrin and held out a hand, saying, "Door to Cernunnos." She fed her power with anger at Orrin and anger at Philip and anger at life. She didn't need any of them. She could make this for herself.

A fiery portal swirled into existence, bleeding embers onto the wet sand. The resonance of it was like nothing she'd ever heard, a kind of ethereal song that threatened to overtake her thoughts.

The world went black.

Chapter 14

"Wake *up*, Tabitha," said a feminine voice nearby.

Someone shook her arm gently. Tabitha was in her bed, in the loft of the church, on top of the blankets. Giada was next to her, worried.

"How did I get here?" She ran a hand through her hair, struggling to figure out where she'd left off in the strange tale her life had become. *Orrin.* A memory of an argument teased the edges of her mind.

"I don't know."

As she rose from the bed, she noticed she still wore the same clothes as the day before. Her bedroom looked just as how she remembered it, the last few unpacked boxes in the corner, a small pile of laundry on the chair. But something didn't feel right.

With Giada following close, she crept down the stairs, scanning the sanctuary for signs of Orrin. Sunlight poured through the tall sanctuary windows, but she couldn't see anything outside the glass. No tree branches, no sky, only a flat, pale light in a sickly shade of yellow.

"What's the last thing you remember?" Tabitha asked Giada.

"A dark forest, a green light behind black trees."

"What about your baby? Did you find her?"

"My baby..." She got a faraway look in her eyes, as if the words triggered a state of confusion.

At the bottom of the stairs, to left and down the hall a few steps, a bloody body lay sprawled across the plush, red rug, one arm propped up, the hand hanging awkwardly as if in some pitiable attempt to reach out for help. Tabitha hurried over to it and found that, just as she feared, it was Philip, his face a bloodied, battered mess. The sound of the gunshot echoed throughout the church, jolting her and Giada. The sound died and came again, louder, an assault on her ears.

This was not her church. None of this was real. Orrin had done as he threatened and trapped her in this false prison. This was his attempt to scare her into submission. It failed.

Fury like she'd never felt before burned through her veins. Staring down at Philip, she felt nothing but anger at these two men. Never again would she allow anyone to make her feel weak.

Tabitha said to Giada, "He wants a lioness. I'll show him a lioness."

She turned back to the sanctuary, stormed over to the spot in which Orrin's door appeared. Blank wall awaited her there, no trace of the ivy or the entrance to his realm.

"Open the damn door, coward."

He didn't answer.

Tabitha did as he'd taught her, gathering the energy around her and summoning it from the depths of her soul. She raised a hand at the wall, envisioned the door for several moments. Nothing happened. She tried again, this time starting with the ivy.

Breathing deep, she channeled her rage into the effort, pushed harder until the edges of her vision darkened. Nothing moved. He was pushing back. Fists clenched at her sides, she roared at the wall.

This place, this sanctuary, was central to Orrin's power. The door belonged to him. What she needed was to create something of her own.

Tabitha returned to bottom of the stairs and the edge of the hallway. Philip's body was gone.

"He was trying to keep me out of the basement." Tabitha started toward the door.

"Wait," Giada said, gently grasping her arm. "We shouldn't go into the basement."

"Why?"

"It's a bad place, remember?"

"In case you haven't noticed, this whole church is a bad place, Giada."

"I know...I just..." Her eyes darted around as she fought to put her worry into words.

"He's weaker down there, isn't he?"

"I don't know what you mean."

"Stay up here if you want. I won't stop you." Tabitha moved on, leaving the ghost standing at the bottom of the loft stairs. Whose side was she on, anyway?

A child appeared between Tabitha and the basement door. Dark hair hanging loose at her shoulders, eyes wide and pleading with Tabitha, Rebecca stared up at her, seeming so small now that one of them had grown. She wore the same pink unicorn shirt and blue jeans that she died in, only these were pure and clean of blood.

"Rebecca?" Unable to stand any longer, she dropped to her knees to hug the child.

"Tabby?" Her voice wasn't quite right, but memory is never perfect. "How long have I been in the dark?"

Tabitha burst into tears. "Too long, honey."

For a heartbeat, she allowed herself to believe that the Rebecca illusion might truly be real. The hope was a fragile, trembling thing, and yet she clung to it, desperate for it to be true. The proximity of it was intoxicating. All she needed to do was believe, and belief, as she knew, could shape reality itself. To linger here, allowing Orrin and Cernunnos to siphon away the essence of her soul, might just be a price worth paying for the dream she had chased for so long.

But *what if*? What if this was the truth, and by doubting, she was casting it all away?

No. She had to live her life. She couldn't play a part in unleashing Cernunnos into the world. Who knew what damage he might do.

"I can't," Tabitha finally said. She released the Rebecca illusion and rose to stand once more. "I'm sorry. I'll find the real you one day."

As Rebecca looked up at her, smiling, Tabitha waved a hand. The illusion vanished in a swirl of white haze, opening a strange wound within Tabitha.

She drew a deep breath and wrenched open the heavy, metal door to the basement. Darkness yawned before her, a hungry maw. Shadows crowded the threshold, pushing back the hallway's feeble light, refusing to let even a sliver of illumination penetrate the inky blackness within.

Behind her, Giada said, "Please don't go."

"Tell me why you don't want me to go. Give me the reason."

"He might hurt my baby."

"Your baby is gone. He never had her," Tabitha snapped, using a harsher tone than she'd intended.

Just like Rebecca, she wanted to add for her own sake.

She turned back to the darkness, took one more deep breath that carried the fragrance of the old church, and stepped in.

Chapter 15

Tabitha ventured into the murk. Nothing before her visible, she felt her way along blindly, stepping on stairs that felt spongy beneath her feet. She fumbled for the light switch, along a wall that felt like decaying skin, fuzzy and wet in places.

A stench of decay filled her lungs, her body rebelling with a fit of coughing. The air was thick and hot, as if she had stepped into the breath of some primordial beast, a creature that lay just beyond the veil, unwilling to fully manifest yet. As she pushed forward, a headache began to coil at the base of her skull, wrapping itself around her thoughts, dragging them into a sluggish spiral.

She struggled for balance on the stairs, each step unstable beneath her feet, the direction of her ascent or descent becoming a treacherous riddle. Up, down—it all blurred together. An urge to turn back gripped her, but which way was back?

Somewhere in the dark beyond, a creature let a long, mournful howl that echoed through the very bones of the church. In her mind, the sound filled the sanctuary and slithered down the hallway, through the open door and into the darkness to reach her.

Then, by some miracle, she was at the bottom of the stairs, where the floor was solid concrete, and the room settled back into some semblance of order and reality. The basement smelled of dust and old paper, and the metal desk sat just as it had that first day, in the middle of the first room, the sad light fixture overhead swinging lazily.

Yet the oasis of reality was incomplete. At the edges, the walls were a swirling, gray haze, not as dark as the murk from which she'd come, but just as thick.

From this haze, a spirit emerged—a woman with the head of a hare, her skin made of white marble veined in grey. She moved toward the desk, paying no mind to Tabitha, and she stood at one side as if waiting.

A second animal spirit, a wolf, came after her and then a third, a bull, until six of them had made a circle around the desk.

Then came the disembodied voice of a man crying out.

"Let go of me! This isn't my time." It was Orrin, angry and fearful.

He appeared on the desk, lying on his back and flailing. Spirit hands darted out to pin down his limbs, because despite his faith and his preaching, Orrin still feared death.

Cernunnos, the stag-headed god himself, materialized behind the bull man and stepped toward the desk, eager to claim the soul promised to him. In his hand, a massive dagger gleamed in the low light. He raised it up and let it drop into Orrin's chest.

Orrin let a strangled cry.

And his captors pulled on his limbs, pulled the man apart where he lay on the desk. And the room dissolved in a frenzy of blood and howling from Orrin and howling from the spirits and Cernunnos.

When the howling finally stopped, the only sound remaining was the drip of blood from the desk to the floor. The spirits stepped back from their work. Cernunnos vanished. The desk vanished and Orrin's mutilated body, until all that remained was the pool of blood and the animal-headed ghosts.

Cernunnos had claimed Orrin's soul before he was ready. It was a betrayal that Tabitha hadn't expected. That was why Orrin had tried to keep her from the basement. His hold was weaker there because that was where he died, where his god had betrayed him, and where he'd lost control over his followers.

Orange light flickered within the center of the pool of blood. It gained life, igniting a swirl within the crimson. It became a molten portal to what Tabitha could only assume was the realm Cernunnos walked.

The spirits lurched forward, reaching for her with pale, eager hands. Tabitha backed away, toward the murk, felt its humid breath on her back.

She had to take a stand. It was the only way out.

"Get back," she commanded, her voice trembling but resolute.

Still, they came for her with their dead eyes and fanged smiles. The bull man clamped a cold, hard hand on her wrist.

She wrenched her arm free. Again, digging deep within her, she drew up the energy she needed, pulling magic from the portal in the middle of the room until flames licked out, toward her.

"Get away from me. You won't take me the way you did him. You're mine to command." The words rang with a power she had always known was there.

A shadow appeared at the center of the portal. Antlers emerged. Cernunnos, the god himself, crawled up from the depths.

His voice boomed, "I am the one you seek. Do you dare command me?"

She faced him, letting the power course through her. "Yes."

He laughed, a deep, resonant sound that shook her to her core. It echoed through the church, mingling with the growl of the portal.

In a motion so fast, she barely detected the movement, he was right in front of her. He gripped her throat, hauled her up into the air.

Terror drove back her resolve. As she stared into the bottomless, black eyes of the god, all that remained was the fear of a prey animal. This was how she would die.

He squeezed, and colors danced in her vision. Breath would not come. There was only agony and fear.

Cold gripped her ankles, and then she was falling. Tabitha dropped through the floor, through a world of shadow, until she landed hard on dirt. She scrambled to her feet, wheeled around, trying to get her bearings.

Light from the windows of the church spilled onto the forest floor. And in that light, a ghostly, green figure dashed toward her in a blur.

"Giada?" Tabitha asked in a voice that refused to climb above a whisper.

It was her friend, the one who had saved her, the one who was there for her all along, running but not fast enough. Cernunnos and his ghostly followers rose up behind her, a tidal wave of anger and spectral energy, and they crashed down on her in a burst of smoke and ember.

Giada screamed.

Tabitha ran.

Chapter 16

A chorus of screams rose in the distance, coming from the direction of the church, growing louder. They closed in, hoof and paw against the earth as Tabitha scrambled through the brush, further and further from the church. The forest itself did its best to ensnare her, branches whipping her face and her bare arms.

Ahead, the way to freedom lie through shadows and cold, autumn air. A vine caught her leg, and she fell hands-first to the ground.

A claw landed on the base of Tabitha's neck and the beginning of her shoulder. It sank deep and then was dragged away, gouging her skin as it yanked off the cross necklace that Constance gave her. A hand encircled her wrist, pulled her up to stand.

His lantern casting wild shadows, Lucas, the man who lived next door, dragged her through the dark forest. Somewhere out of sight, Jackal barked wildly.

They ran for several minutes until the back of Lucas' house appeared in front of them. A motion-sensing light clicked on as he ran her up three steps and through a tilting screened-in porch.

He flung her inside, grabbed Jackal next, and spun back around in a graceful motion to reach into a bucket sitting on a counter next to the back door. With his other hand, he slammed the door and turned the deadbolt. He poured a handful of white powder across the threshold. He stopped then, out of breath, waiting.

Something large crashed into the other side of the door, rattled it, and then pounded. Then came a sound like a roar and a screech blending together. It died away, leaving an eerie silence in its wake.

"It will hold," Lucas said, more to himself than to Tabitha.

"What is that?" she asked.

"Salt." He pointed to the white stuff he'd poured on the floor. "There's some at every door and on every windowsill. Should keep them out." After a few seconds of silence, he nodded slowly and then turned. "Come on."

He toted the lantern with him as he moved through an avocado green and white kitchen, to a dining room. The place smelled like cooked food and dust and the woodsy scent of the man himself.

He motioned to a long, farmhouse table. "Wait here. I'll be right back."

"Where are you going?" Tabitha asked, panic rising anew at the thought of being alone this soon after the chase.

"I'm grabbing the first aid kit."

Heat spread from her shoulder as blood soaked through the remnants of her sleeve. The collar of her shirt was wet. She covered the gouges with one hand and immediately discovered that the bleeding was worse than she'd thought, the wounds deeper. She imagined those mossy, marble claws sinking into her flesh and shuddered.

"How did you know about the salt?" she asked Lucas once he returned. He sat sideways in the chair next to her, gingerly dabbing at her skin with a rag.

He shrugged. "When you deal with this stuff as long as I have, you do your homework. You probably need some stitches, but we might want to put that off until morning. They won't let us leave." He hit an especially tender spot, which sent a fresh shot of pain through her, and she winced. He said, "Sorry."

He started work on the bandages and tape, looking at the wound from different angles before deciding how to tackle it.

Tabitha asked, "How did you know to come find me?"

"No offense, Ms. Mainwater, but you and those demons aren't the quietest neighbors I've ever had. I see you've met the animal spirits. They prowl the forest at night. I'm pretty sure they're the ones who ruined my family's land. I can keep them off the property with some well-placed runes, but the ivy always finds its way in. Never seen them riled up like this, though. What'd you do?"

Tabitha scoffed. "Pretty sure they were riled up well before I got here. It's complicated."

"Try me."

"Orrin wants to bring an old god back to the mortal plane."

"Cernunnos?"

"Yeah."

"What does that have to do with you?"

Tabitha let an ironic laugh. "Apparently, my soul burns bright. So ridiculous. As far as I can tell, they want to use me as some kind of battery."

Lucas shook his head. "Figures."

"Why do you say that?"

"Orrin was always good at manipulating people. You fell for the same lines he fed his followers."

"I'm a medium. I can do things that regular people can't. I am different. Why is this difficult for you to believe?"

"I'm just saying that part of his spiel was to make people feel like they were superior in some kind of way and that he could enhance their natural abilities. Naivety is nothing to be ashamed of."

Her face hot with embarrassment, Tabitha stood up. "I am not naive. I've trained with the best mediums I could find. I can do things you can't even dream of."

Lucas rolled his eyes. "Alright, Ms. Mainwater, simmer down. We're all special here." He left the table to go to the kitchen. As he stared out the window at the field out back, he took items from a tin on the counter and absentmindedly rolled a joint and lit it. "They're in rare form tonight."

Tabitha joined him at the window. Outside, about twenty of the spirits frolicked through the field, dancing in a ballet beneath the starry night sky. She took the joint as Lucas offered it, and the smoke stung her lungs.

"All I wanted to do was find my friend on the other side," she said.

"Well, look at the bright side. You have plenty of new friends."

"Very funny."

"We have to let go of people we lose. They move on, and so should we. If you had let go of your friend, we wouldn't be surrounded by malevolent spirits. It's selfishness."

"You don't understand."

"Understand what? Loss?"

"Loss so profound that it takes root in your heart."

"Let me tell you about loss." He snatched the joint from her hand and took a deep drag. "When I was sixteen, my father got tired of struggling to grow crops on this cursed land. He drove his truck out to the field and shot himself. My mother found him."

"Oh, my God. I'm so sorry, Lu—"

"Like you, my mother also couldn't let go. She called in medium after medium, trying to find my father in the afterlife. All were hacks."

"I'm sorry that happened to you. We aren't all hacks."

"She kept seeing ghosts in the fields, those things. And people around town told her she was crazy. Then she got sick. The longer those things stayed in the fields, the sicker she got, until right before my eighteenth birthday, when she died. You see, I think the mediums, as useless as they were, somehow attracted those monsters to our fields. Nothing good comes of talking to the dead. Nothing."

"Not all spirits are bad. Giada...oh, God, Giada." In the chaos, she'd almost forgotten her friend. Tabitha started toward the back door.

Lucas gently stopped her with a hand on her arm. "If you run out now, you're going to get eaten alive. We need some kind of plan, preferably one that involves sunlight."

He was right, so she listened, and she was glad to let someone else have control for a while. Too much was happening. He gave her some beer and some leftover lasagna from the fridge, and then he coaxed her to the couch, gave her a couple of blankets, and told her to get some rest.

Chapter 17

Her shoulder was cold when she woke to daylight streaming through the gauzy, living room curtains. The light was strangely warm, tinted a shade of amber that gave the room an unreal quality.

It was too bright to be dawn. She'd slept late. She got up from the couch too fast, and the floor tilted under her feet. The bandage on her neck and shoulder was soaked with blood.

"Lucas!" she yelled, and he appeared at the edge of a hallway, looking as confused and disoriented as she felt.

"What is this?" he asked.

"I don't know. Is it dawn?"

He glanced at the clock on his way to the window. "Not even close." It was 3:00 am.

They pulled back the curtains to find the yard had transformed. Beneath a bright amber sky, trees in flaming shades of autumn glowed as if gilded. Leaves fell, turning over in the air before alighting on vividly green grass. The world looked as if someone had cranked the saturation ten notches too high, and in that world, spirit statues crowded Lucas McGuire's front lawn.

Ten of them stood in staggered formation, striking strangely dramatic poses that echoed the relief on the wall in Orrin's hallway. A few looked toward the sky, holding hands in front of their beast faces as if terrified of what God had in store for them. A couple were on their knees as if acting out some sort of contrition. Others stood ready for battle against one another, fists raised. One held a spear. If not for the threat the scene carried, it might've been beautiful.

"What are they doing?" Lucas asked.

"They want us to come out. Maybe they're waiting."

The amber sky dimmed and brightened, dimmed and brightened, and then a bruise color spread through it, stealing its warmth completely. Then came rain, a shower descending like a hawk on prey, drenching the leaves and the statues.

The ghosts moved, beginning with a pair of hyena-headed women. Next came a fox, a bear, a raven, and a handful of coyotes approached the house in slow, jerking movements.

"You said you salted the front door, right?" Tabitha asked Lucas.

"Yeah, the windows, too."

Then, over the sound of the rain, she heard it in the distance, the wail of an infant. The cry seemed to grow louder, get closer, and Tabitha had a vision of Giada carrying a baby through the storm.

"Giada," Tabitha said under her breath.

Lucas gently grasped her by the shoulders and turned her to face him. He said, "They're using her to manipulate you. You can't let them. We have to stay inside no matter what. If you step over that line, there's no coming back. Please tell me you understand."

The wailing baby drew closer.

Lucas shook her a little.

"I understand," she said quickly. She returned to the window to find a veined marble hyena face right on the other side of the glass. She stumbled backward, the sound of the thing's laughter following her.

Lucas parted the curtains, pulling them wide.

More spirits had assembled on the porch, and they stood idly, a coyote woman reclining on the railing like a big cat. Rain still drummed the yard behind them, relentless and thick, and from deep within the haze it made, a figure walked into view.

"Shit," Tabitha said as she retreated once more.

"Is it your friend?" Lucas asked.

"Yes." Tears warmed her cheeks. "What am I supposed to do? I can't just let them have her."

"We'll figure it out. You need to be strong. Remember what I said."

Thunder rumbled in the distance, a deep, hungry sound. A bundled infant in her arms, Giada, soaked by the rain, crossed the front yard, ascended the steps.

"They can't cross the salt line, right?"

"Yes, but—"

Before he could finish, Tabitha wrenched the front door open, a flood of harsh daylight spilling over her. Giada stood unnervingly close, right on the other side of the salt line. Slowly, reluctantly, she lifted her gaze from the baby in her arms to meet Tabitha's.

"Isn't it wonderful?" Giada asked. Her eyes had turned to marble, just like the spirits in the yard. Tabitha was losing her.

Thunder rumbled again, and the rain picked up. Wind pushed its way into the house, carrying an acrid, burning smell with it.

She said, "Giada, you have to get out of here. Run, now. We can find each other later."

"Why would I do that? Cernunnos has given me everything I ever wanted. He is a god of life and death. He blesses us."

Tabitha turned to Lucas. "Can we let her in without the rest of them?"

He shook his head no. "Come on. We have to shut the door."

At her feet, the wind from the storm was eroding the salt line. She needed more time.

"Tabitha, close the door," he said as he reached for the small bucket of salt on the table.

"Please, Giada. Take the baby if you have to, but leave. Just go."

A burst of wind and rain hit her, and without looking down, she knew their salt line was gone. The house tumbled into darkness.

Chapter 18

"Lucas?" Tabitha said.

He cried out, and there was a sickening thud like a body hitting the floor. Then she was tugged by her arms, shoved from behind into the torrent, and the storm whirled around her. She couldn't see, could only feel the force of them moving her. She lost her footing, but they didn't let her fall. She tried to call for Lucas again, but the rain and the wind stole her breath and her voice.

The next she knew, they cast her down on rough carpet the color of dried blood and slammed a door behind her. She sat up. Scrapes burned her palms, knees, and elbows.

None of Orrin's minions had stayed behind. Lucas wasn't there, either. She was alone in a decrepit shack that she didn't recognize. It smelled of dust and decay, of things long abandoned.

The floor slanted away from her, toward the other side of the room, where a wall was open to a forest enveloped in night. Leaves there were summer-lush. Crickets sang. Some other night creature shrilled. No escape from the nightmare lay that direction; she knew, but her only chance for survival was to win their game. She got up, dusted herself off.

The edge of the floor dug into the earth as if someone had intended to use it as a shovel but stopped. She made her way that direction, stepping into the summer forest. The air was fresh and wild. Absinthe green light shone from somewhere beyond the trees. Where was she supposed to go?

The baby cried in the distance, the sound joining the crickets and the other nocturnal creatures. She headed that direction, following a dirt trail that Orrin likely manifested to lead her the way he wanted her to go.

Ghosts moved through the trees on either side of the trail. They kept pace with her, carving paths of their own that ventured closer and closer to hers.

Worse, their heads all remained turned toward her. They stared hungrily with those blank eyes as they prowled cautiously through the underbrush, their gazes never deviating from her. At word one from Orrin, they could tear her apart, and they'd be all too happy to do it. They wanted her to join them in death.

The baby cry died suddenly, broken off and replaced by a heavy silence. Tabitha broke into a run, following the trail, and Orrin's menagerie kept pace. The dirt trail veered left and then up a small rise. It narrowed and then ended at a clearing.

Beneath a patch of black sky pierced by silvery moonbeams, a rattlesnake woman sat with her legs tucked around one side. Like the others, she was naked and pale. Unlike the others, a faint orange light played across her marble skin as if a fire burned nearby. Unlike the others, she didn't belong here.

"Giada?" Tabitha asked. No part of this spirit physically resembled her friend. Even the energy of the creature felt different, predatory. The sense of familiarity shouldn't have tugged at Tabitha the way it did. Still, she had no doubt.

Giada rose to stand, approached in a stride that was more prowl than walk. The lifeless eyes were the worst part, blank like the others, dead like the others. And the rattlesnake hood was spread wide in a threat. Giada stopped a couple of feet away.

Tabitha resisted the urge to run. Maybe there was still a way. Maybe she could save Giada, pull her back from Orrin's grasp.

Other ghosts filed into the clearing behind Tabitha, moving to form a half-circle behind her, moving to block her retreat. They didn't have to. She didn't plan on running.

"We can go back," Tabitha said. "We can find our way back to the church, but you have to fight this. You can't let them win."

The rattlesnake head tilted slightly as if the thing that had once been her friend studied her. Then, in a flash, the fangs were sinking into the wounded parts of Tabitha's neck and shoulder.

Blinding pain moved through every part of her with a weight that seemed to crush her heart. It brought fire to her veins, and she knew the bite was venomous.

She had no breath to scream, no strength with which to push back. Her legs went weak beneath her, but they held her in place. Hands were on her back and her arms. One from behind pulled her hair taut, the better to let the venom do its work.

Then, after too much time in that hell, they released her. Tabitha fell to her hands and knees in the dirt. As she watched her blood drip onto the ground, the crickets and the rest of the night creatures made their return, their songs pulsing with the strange rhythm of her heart.

Poison coursed through her, hot and stinging, blurring her vision, bringing nausea. Could she bleed the poison out? If she lost enough blood, just the right amount, maybe it wouldn't kill her.

She collected her wits and sat upright. The ground swayed, and she had to catch herself to keep from falling.

The sky flickered from black back to green as she stood. She wheeled around in a clumsy circle to find the ghosts retreating into the trees, their work apparently done.

Giada had vanished. The hyenas laughed, a high, cruel sound. Two of them crouched and then jumped straight up into the tree branches. Most of them took to the shadows, dashing off in a whisper of leaves and cracking of twigs.

Chapter 19

Somewhere out of sight, Giada cried. She sounded like herself. Hope swelled in Tabitha and once more, she headed the direction Orrin wanted her to go.

This time, there was no trail. Trees crowded, threatening to close her in. Thorny vines crawled across the ground, snagging her pants like tiny claws trying to hold her back. The place smelled of decay.

A green sky pressed closer, desperate to show her that the ghosts had not left. They lounged on branches like jungle cats, or they dangled by arms or legs. A horse man appeared several times, hanging by a noose, his dead eyes wide, mouth hanging open.

All the while, blood streamed down Tabitha's neck and shoulder, mixing with the sweat now surfacing on every inch of her skin. The poison had given her a fever. She vomited once, twice, and pushed through, unsure of what was real if any of it was. Tabitha stopped to lean on a tree and tried to blink her vision back into focus.

Giada stopped crying.

A shack appeared several yards ahead. The structure leaned and buckled in places. Colonies of corpse-white fungus dappled the deep red walls. Small candles burned in the front windows. There was no door, only an open threshold.

The trees constricted. Slowly but surely, they were pushing her toward the shack. And in its eagerness, the sky burned an even brighter shade of absinthe green.

Tabitha stumbled forward and through the doorway. At first, the room was dark. Then, as if someone turned up a lamp, warm light spread, illuminating burgundy walls, antique furniture, and a fireplace that smelled of soot. To her right, a grandfather clock ticked louder than it should've, and the sound was angry.

On the other side of the window on the back wall, a man hung from a long branch, his fingers curled around the noose on his neck, legs kicking frantically.

"Lucas!" Tabitha slapped her palm to the glass.

Hyena and coyote spirits were gathered on the ground beneath him. One wore a blindfold and held a stick, and another one was spinning him around and around. They planned to use him as a piñata.

She shouted at the ceiling, "Let him go."

Delicate piano music descended on the room, coming from all around, echoing in her feverish mind. Then came the voice of the architect himself, speaking from nowhere and everywhere.

"Now, now, little cow." His tone was smooth and controlled. "I can release him with a snap of my fingers. You know that I can, but I need something from you first, my lioness."

"I'm not becoming one of those things," she said.

"Those *things?* My children are beautiful. They're flawless. You should be so lucky. Pledge yourself to Cernunnos. Give yourself to us the way the others have."

"No."

Outside, Lucas screamed. The blindfolded coyote hit him with the stick and then jabbed it into his gut, cutting off the scream.

She turned to leave, but the open threshold was gone. In its place was a mirror image of the other wall, minus the window. Ivy grew down from the ceiling, coiling and twisting to the sound of the piano and the rabid tick of the clock.

She needed to get out of there. She had to gain control, somehow. She grabbed a fireplace poker and raised it over her shoulder like a bat. She loosened her grip, fully aware that the window probably wouldn't break. Orrin wouldn't let it be that easy, but she'd try, anyway.

Tabitha hit it once, twice, harder each time, her rage finding its way into her arms. When she was tired and angry enough, she hurled the poker at the fireplace, where it struck the brick and landed on the wooden floor.

Tabitha felt sick and boiling hot like she might vomit again. She bent over, one hand on her knee, the other on the wall to keep her from falling over. The venom burned through her, making everything worse.

"It's not real," she insisted to herself. "It's not real, and I can fight it." If she was going to survive, she needed both those things to be true.

She willed coolness into her veins. She willed her sense of balance to return, and it did. The shack settled around her.

Next came the window. She focused on it, willing it to break. All she had to do was think the right way, want it the right way; she was sure. She conjured a vision of the glass shattering and the pieces falling to the floor. With every ounce of strength she could muster in the moment, she drove her will toward it.

Nothing happened. In the distance, Lucas' shouts were fading. He was losing the battle for his life. She couldn't bear to look at him again, so she turned back to the room.

The clock continued ticking. Piano music played on faintly. Orrin's gaze coiled around her as his ivy draped itself down the walls. She hated this place, hated him, hated her own weakness.

Tabitha walked over to the grandfather clock and heaved it over onto the floor, satisfied with the ensuing sounds of breakage and the scattering of small parts. The ticking ceased. Wiping sweat from her forehead with the back of her arm, she smiled.

She turned back to the window.

"Delusional child," he said, and then he laughed. "Do you really think it's that easy? I had to die to become a god. Even if I killed you right now, your strength would not be enough."

Behind her, the grandfather clock reversed. It rose, pieces levitating back into place as it did so. When it was done, the maddening ticktock of the thing returned.

Rage pulsed through her, and she roared at the clock and at Orrin. It moved through her in waves, fueled by adrenaline. She focused on the window with new intensity. A crack formed. An inch, two inches, a shimmering, pale thing that split into branches.

In a flash of white, sharp pain knifed through Tabitha's head. She cried out and bent over to keep from passing out. She gathered herself up to try again, but the ivy had overgrown the window. It formed a curtain over the wall, the heavy fragrance of it settling over her like a cloud.

Pale as death hands shot out and grabbed her, yanked her through so fast that the leaves whipped her skin. Then she found herself in a tunnel of green. The ghost pulled her through a deep patch of it, somehow keeping enough leaves between them that Tabitha couldn't see who or what was pulling her.

At the edge of the leaves, the back of the rattlesnake hood came into view.

They emerged a few yards from the hanging tree, where Lucas still kicked and flailed and shouted and wheezed. The ghosts had given up their piñata game to tug on his legs instead.

If Lucas really hung from the tree, with his full weight dragging him down, there was no way he would've survived that long. Did that mean this was an illusion or did it mean that Orrin could somehow keep him alive despite the torment?

The rattlesnake shoved her to her knees in the dirt.

Orrin materialized in front of her, but he had changed. He had become a blend of him and Cernunnos, antlers sprouting from his head, eyes black as deepest dark. He brandished a dagger, saying nothing, at first. Then he turned.

"Cut him down," he said to his servants, who did as he commanded. Then he spoke to Tabitha. "If you won't give yourself to me willingly, some coercion is in order."

A hyena woman and a coyote woman forced Lucas to his knees on the ground. His neck was red and raw, blood seeping through in places, and his face was a mask of fear, all thought hollowed out by desperation for survival.

Beast Orrin said, "If you want this man to continue on his mortal path...well, you know what to do." He twirled the knife and sauntered the few steps over to Lucas. Then he added, "Perhaps a few more screams will convince you, perhaps the delicious kind that people let loose while being skinned alive. I bet you'd give me anything, then."

Branches overhead creaked under the weight of many animal-headed spirits. And the ivy crept everywhere in a whisper, growing faster than it ever had.

This was never the way to reach Rebecca. If she was going to defeat Cernunnos and Orrin, she needed to stop believing that any part of their power would help her.

Lucas' words from the night before echoed in her mind. *"We have to let go of people we lose. They move on, and so should we. If you had let go of your friend, we wouldn't be surrounded by malevolent spirits. It's selfishness."*

He was right. Of course, he was. This twilight realm between worlds held no answers. It was a place of shadows and echoes, not of resolutions. Cernunnos, Orrin, and the spirits had to be driven forward, into the next unknown, the beyond where their true fates waited.

Drawing in the spirit energy around her, she conjured one last portal. She wove it from darkness and peace, stars and belonging, the fabric of fate itself. The portal opened before her, vast, swallowing pieces of Beast Orrin's illusion as he bellowed with rage.

The spirits tried, unsuccessfully, to cling to each other, to cling to trees. They reached for their god with fingers that closed on nothing. Fate swept them away just like it always intended, and they tumbled into the beyond.

"Stop her!" Orrin shouted in a layered voice that belonged to both him and the god possessing him.

She closed her eyes and fed the portal with all she had, losing the screams in the roar of the wind and howling from Cernunnos. This was the end for all of the dead who inhabited the church, including Giada, but Tabitha had to let her go, just like she had to let Rebecca and her father go, because moving on was part of life.

The last she saw, Cernunnos and Orrin plunged into the portal as one, their screams cutting through the sound of wind and time. In the end, all went dark. Time passed there; she was sure. It stretched into an ocean, and she sank into it, cradled in its currents.

Chapter 20

"This was all I could get on short notice." Constance stood with Tabitha, Lucas, and Jackal on Lucas' back porch, watching as four women moved along the edges of the overgrown field, burning sage and nailing totems into the trunks of every few trees.

"I'm sure they're doing great," Tabitha said. "It's probably overkill at this point. I haven't felt any presences since that night." She ran a hand over the ache in her bandaged shoulder and neck. Unfortunately, the injury hadn't departed with the spirits that caused it, and she never did find the necklace.

"I'm going to have to learn to plant crops." Lucas said.

"I'll help." Tabitha smiled over at him.

After what she'd gone through, some people would've hightailed it out of there at the first opportunity. But if she did that, if she sold the church, someone else would've bought it, and should Orrin or Cernunnos find a way back, they'd be done for. Instead, she chose to become a guardian of the place. For as long as she lived, she would hold the spiritual line there, and she was not afraid.

She'd heard rumors about Philip, her abusive ex. In the day or two after she'd purged the dead from the grounds, someone found him walking along a country road a few miles away, no shoes, no car. He was delirious and dehydrated, claiming that he'd escaped a ghost world, but there were no wounds other than the marks on his feet. After that, he left for his parents' house in Tennessee.

Orrin had blurred the lines between reality and illusion. He was a master of it, after all. The best she could guess, Orrin had held Philip somewhere in his realm. What had he seen while he was there? What had he endured? She hoped it was unpleasant.

Despite all that Philip had done to her, she was glad he was alive. Living with the weight of someone's death on her shoulders would've been worse, that and the constant fear of being caught. Instead, what she had now was a sense of peace like she'd never felt before.

Later, back in her church, with the light of autumn dusk streaming through the windows, she sat down at her easel to paint. Without a photo reference, the sketch had taken her a while to complete, but she finally got it right.

Like the paintings of Rebecca and her father, this one was for her. A light pencil version of Giada smiled out from the white canvas, her angel wings white and folded neatly behind her. In her arms, she cradled her bundled infant daughter.

For years, they were near-constant companions. Now the loss of her had left an open wound in Tabitha. The shared glances, the conversations and advice, all that remained were memories. And whenever the tears welled up again, she insisted to herself that this was for the best. It was the natural order of things. If fate offered a chance, they'd see each other again.

Now, Tabitha would find fulfillment on the mortal plane. If the need arose, she would again venture beyond the veil, but for the moment, she would relish in the warmth of the sun on her face and the quiet that settled over the church once the curse was lifted. For now, she would live.

The End

Note from the author:

Thank you for reading *Church of Shadows*!

If you enjoyed this story, I'd be so grateful if you took a moment to leave a review at your favorite book retailer's website. Reviews help other readers discover the book and make a huge difference for indie authors like me. Whether it's a few words or a full reflection, your thoughts mean the world—and help keep the stories coming!

Thank you for your support! <3

Lea Ryan

PS: My blog and more information about my work can be found at www.LeaRyan.com[1].

---

1. http://www.learyan.com/